Don't Call Me A Ghost!

Growing Up With Albinism Around the World

Don't Call Me A Ghost!

Growing Up With
Albinism Around the World

Cynthia H. Roman, Ed.D.

ISBN 978-1-62806-346-2   (paperback | print)

Library of Congress Control Number 2022902700

Published by
Salt Water Media
29 Broad Street, Suite 104
Berlin, MD 21811
www.saltwatermedia.com

Cover design by Allison Melfa

Contents

Acknowledgements

Thank you…

To my loving husband, Jim Wieboldt, who made sure I was clear and concise when my personal experience with albinism caused me to make assumptions about what my reader would know. He always asked great questions and his "what-ifs?" never failed to steer me in a better direction.

To my editor, Bill Cecil. His "old school" process was ideal for this "old school" writer!

To Allison Melfa for the fantastic cover art. I am so fortunate to have found such a talented artist.

To my friends and fellow writers in the First Saturday Writer's Group of Berlin, Maryland, who read many drafts of the short stories in this book. Their skills, talent, and varied perspectives helped me make significant improvements in the structure and organization of the book, as well as help me be a better writer.

To the good folks of Salt Water Media, my publisher. This is the third book they've published for me and I so appreciate their expertise and accessibility.

To Virginia Bianco-Mathis, my long-time special friend and former business partner. She gave me invaluable feedback about my original concept, as well as the content of the short stories.

Preface

If you are a Person with Albinism (PWA), this book is for you. If you have a friend or family member who is a PWA, this book is for you. If you are a young adult who doesn't know much about albinism, this book is for you. And finally, if you care about human rights around the world, this book is for you.

I am a PWA. When I was growing up, I knew that I had fair skin, very blonde hair and somewhat weak eyesight. But the word albinism was never spoken in my home. I never understood why I didn't tan or why my eyeglasses didn't completely correct my eyesight. As a young child, I went through a battery of vision tests at our local university hospital, but I was never told why and apparently nothing ever came of them.

Now I am in my sixties and retired. I have only recently been diagnosed with oculocutaneous albinism (OCA) by both my ophthalmologist and my dermatologist. I've led an active life and I've enjoyed a degree of career success. But I've also suffered chronic migraine headaches and I can't count how many skin cancer lesions I've had removed.

As a retired university professor, I have experience writing books and articles for academic purposes. Since I retired, I now write books and short stories that explore my more creative side. *Don't Call Me A Ghost!* is a book of short stories that falls into the category of *realistic fiction*.

Realistic fiction explores imaginary characters and situations that depict the real world around us—both local and global. It often focuses on themes of growing up and coping with personal and social problems. The characters and scenarios in this book are fictionalized but they are based on research and reality.

Don't Call Me A Ghost! consists of twelve short stories about growing up with albinism around the world. Each chapter is a story of a child in a different country. From China to the United States, from Africa to South America, albinism exists all over the world. I chose the countries based on their availability of information, the factual basis for the story, and how the albinism experience differs from other countries. For example, while many countries in Africa present serious challenges for people with albinism, I chose to write about Tanzania and South Africa in order to describe two significant but different sets of national and cultural issues. Albinism is a genetic condition that occurs in some countries more than others. Some countries provide a positive environment and numerous resources to assist people with albinism; others do not. These stories are written for the young adult reader, but many adults may find the stories both compelling and enlightening.

A separate chapter in this book provides the reader with up-to-date information about albinism: what it is, what it isn't, and how it is treated. The last section in the book provides a list of resources about albinism around the world. My hope is that this book will help us all respond to this genetic condition with more accurate information, more compassion, and more resources to help everyone with albinism, regardless of where they live.

Short Stories
About
Growing Up With Albinism

Australia

| Cassie |

"Mrs. Wilson? G'day! This is Julia Smith, Cassie's teacher. I'm calling because I have some concerns about Cassie. Do you have a few minutes to talk?"

Seven-year-old Cassie was drawing quietly at the kitchen table when Mrs. Smith called. As she listened to her mother's phone conversation, she soon realized that the caller was her teacher and they were talking about her.

"What do you mean, it is difficult to meet Cassie's needs in the classroom? My Cassie is a little Aussie battler! And a school for the blind is not appropriate for her level of vision impairment," Cassie's mother said to Mrs. Smith with a note of alarm in her voice. "If she sits in the front row and if you try to write a little bigger on the blackboard, Cassie will do just fine. She has glasses. Is she wearing them in the classroom?"

At this, Cassie got up from the kitchen table and walked over to her mother.

"Mum?" Cassie interrupted her mother's phone conversation and tugged on her blouse.

"I sit in the back because the other kids make fun of me. So I sit where they can't see me. I do wear my glasses though. Emily helps me when I can't see the board." Emily was Cassie's best friend and they were in the same class.

Mrs. Wilson shushed her daughter and returned to her phone conversation with the teacher.

"Mrs. Smith, Cassie just told me that she sits in the back of the classroom because the other kids make fun of her. Did you realize that my daughter is being bullied in your classroom?" Mrs. Wilson's tone had gone from alarmed to angry. And as Mrs. Wilson spoke to Cassie's teacher, her face turned red.

Mrs. Smith replied quickly. "Mrs. Wilson, I reprimanded a student in the class who called Cassie Casper and ghost. Cassie is a sweet girl but she needs to learn how to stand up for herself. Those are real-world skills. She tends to try to hide from the other children. I tried to get her to sit up front in our classroom but she wanted to sit in back with her mate, Emily."

Cassie's mother responded tersely. "Mrs. Smith, I am very disappointed that you seem to allow students to call Cassie names and get away with it. I understand that picking on people who are different is a reality but teaching compassion and respect is part of your job. Allowing children to call Cassie Casper or ghost is ugly and unacceptable. As for Cassie's vision, she has a few problems but she is not legally blind. I take her to her ophthalmologist every six months to update her eyeglass prescription. You need to make sure she sits in the front row and that the other children treat her with respect, no matter where she sits."

Mrs. Smith ended the phone conversation by suggesting a personal conference among herself, Cassie's parents, and the school principal to discuss Cassie's educational future. That night, after Cassie had gone to bed, her mother and father talked well into the evening. The second grade teacher's words and attitude toward their young daughter were alarming and they were unprepared for anyone to suggest that Cassie might not be successful in school. They realized that if anyone was going to advocate for Cassie's well-being and rights, it would have to be them.

From the time Cassie was born, her parents had supported her in every way they could. But they never thought of her as disabled. Quite the contrary, they encouraged her to play with the other children in the neighborhood and to develop a sense of independence. Cassie learned how to play hide and seek with the other children, and she wanted to go the playground almost every day after school. She loved the swings and the jungle gym equipment. Cassie began seeing an ophthalmologist by the time she was three years old and she had surgery to improve her involuntary side-to-side eye movements, called nystagmus. With her prescription glasses, Cassie could read her books, as long as she was up close to the print. While she would never have perfect vision, Cassie's parents and her ophthalmologist believed that their daughter would succeed in the classroom.

Cassie's first year in school had gone well. She seemed happy and she met Emily, who would soon become her best mate. More importantly, her parents never received any worrying communication from Cassie's school or teacher.

During the next week following the phone call with Cassie's teacher, Mr. and Mrs. Wilson developed a plan of action for supporting their daughter at school. They were pleased with the outcome of the school conference. The principal agreed to ensure that teachers would have zero tolerance for bullying toward anyone, including Cassie. Because Cassie's vision impairment was not severe enough to qualify her as disabled, there was no further suggestion that Cassie attend a school for the blind. Finally, the Wilsons requested the opportunity to give a workshop to the faculty on how to support children with albinism. The principal welcomed the offer and scheduled the workshop for the next month.

Despite the success of the school conference, the experience marked a turning point. Nothing had prepared Cassie or her parents for the ignorance about albinism they encountered at her school and the bullying from the other children. And so began a journey for Cassie that forced her to grapple with what it was to have albinism in a world where being different often meant isolation and cruelty. Even worse, Cassie began to internalize the judgmental attitudes.

By the time she started secondary school, Cassie felt fundamentally different from others. She resented being born with poor eyesight, pale skin, and white hair. She didn't like who she was. She became painfully shy and rarely socialized with other kids. Only Emily, Cassie's long-time friend, seemed to understand and accept her.

One day after school, Cassie and Emily watched a video of the movie, "The Da Vinci Code", in which the villain, Silas, is portrayed as an evil monk with albinism. Emily—always protective of her mate's feelings—suggested they stop watching, but Cassie was fascinated.

"Why does the evil character have to have albinism? That is so unfair," Cassie exclaimed to Emily.

Shocked by the portrayal of someone with her genetic condition, Cassie began to do research on how albinism has been depicted in film and literature. Her discovery of the evil albino stereotype throughout history and culture resulted in a term paper for her senior Honors English class. When her paper was submitted to a national student writing contest and won first prize, Cassie's view of herself began to shift. Her lack of self-acceptance morphed into a determination that she would not let her condition, or others' attitudes about people with her condition, limit her.

Cassie's college days flew by at the University of Melbourne. She earned her BA degree in English and Theatre Studies, becoming an expert on how disabilities are depicted in media. When she graduated, Cassie was hired at IDEAS, (Information on Disability Education & Awareness Services) a national advocacy organization in Australia. IDEAS's purpose is to provide access to independent information and opportunities for people with disabilities, their supporters, and the community to reach their full potential.

One day while visiting her parents, Cassie decided to

also visit her childhood primary school, hoping to find Mrs. Smith, her second grade teacher, still there. She headed down the hallway just as school finished the day. She saw an older, grayer Mrs. Smith, loaded down with a stack of papers, locking her classroom door.

Cassie called out before Mrs. Smith walked in the opposite direction toward the parking lot. "Hi Mrs. Smith!"

The teacher turned around and waited for Cassie to draw near. Mrs. Smith looked puzzled.

"Do you remember me, the student with albinism? I was in your class seventeen years ago. I'm Cassie Wilson."

Mrs. Smith broke into a wide grin and dropped her papers all over the floor. She grabbed Cassie and gave her a big hug.

"Oh my goodness, Cassie! You're all grown up and so beautiful! I will never forget you. You and your parents taught me how important it is to show compassion and respect for anyone who is a little or a lot different! You made a huge difference in the way I teach—in fact, the way I look at people now. I'm so glad I can tell you that in person. Now tell me all about yourself. I bet you are a huge success in your life!"

Cassie bent down to help pick up Mrs. Smith's papers and replied, "It's been quite a journey. Let's go sit on the front steps and I'll tell you all about it!"

Brazil

| Antonia |

Maria sat at her front window, working at her sewing machine. Business in her sewing and mending business was good right now and she couldn't afford any time away from the mountain of torn jeans and ripped children's swimsuits the beach hotels sent her from their tourist customers. It was high season in the coastal city of Salvador, Brazil, after all, and Maria welcomed the work.

But it was 3:30 in the afternoon and she looked up from her work for the expected arrival of Antonia from school. It was a daily ritual for Maria to greet her beloved 16-year-old granddaughter with a Coke and a plate of *Acaraje*, fried fritters filled with flour-based fish paste, and fresh fruit. Antonia loved the spicy fritters, which had been a family staple since Maria's own childhood.

But today, when Maria looked out of the window, she was startled to see that Antonia was not alone as she walked up the dirt road toward their house. A boy was walking with her and the two teenagers were talking and laughing together. Maria felt the beginning of a knot in her stomach, but she got up and went to open the door.

"Avo," Antonia said, greeting her grandmother in Portuguese. "This is Jose, my friend from school." She sounded comfortable in making the introduction to her grandmother, not the least bit nervous. Maria's knot went away.

"I'm happy to meet you, Jose. Come in with Antonia and have something to eat."

Maria smiled, thinking this boy might be different from the other kids in Antonia's school, or the bullies in the neighborhood. Or even from the people who rudely just stared at Antonia's pale skin and light yellow hair.

Jose looked at the little table in the main room, filled with a big plate of Acaraje, fruit, and one can of Coke. He glanced at Antonia, but of course, she wasn't able to see the table clearly including the fact that a second can of Coke was needed. However, Maria did notice and she quickly said, "I'll get another Coke from the refrigerator."

"Thank you," Jose replied.

He lightly touched Antonia's elbow and they walked together toward the table.

"Avo, Jose is going to read a story to me from our literature book since my eyes are hurting and I have a little headache," Antonia said. "Then, if my eyes feel better, I'm going to help him with his algebra. We make a good team."

"That's good. I'm going back to my sewing machine. I'll be up to midnight if I don't keep working on all these orders."

Over the next hour and a half, Maria tried to stay focused on her sewing but couldn't help but glance up occasionally at the teens across the room. Antonia sat with her eyes closed as she listened to Jose read. Then, she used her magnifying glass to help him with his algebra problems. It all seemed so easy and even natural.

As Maria made her way through broken swimsuit straps and missing buttons, she thought back on what it was like to raise Antonia, a black Brazilian girl with albinism. She thought about the fateful night only a week after Antonia's birth. The baby's father came to the house where they all lived—drunk as usual— and screamed at Antonia's mother, Lucia.

"I know that white baby isn't mine. You cheated on me, you whore!"

He left that night and none of them ever saw him again. Like so many black Brazilian men who had little education, Antonia's father knew nothing about albinism. He didn't know that he could be a carrier of the albinism genes without displaying any of the characteristics. He had dark hair and dark skin, as did Lucia. He knew he was descended from the African slaves brought to Brazil to work on the sugar cane plantations. He worked as a construction laborer, and like others in the Brazilian culture, he bragged to his buddies about his sexual prowess. He couldn't wait to show off his offspring. When Antonia was born, he was shocked to his core. He got drunk in a hurry. His rage only increased with each passing day.

To be honest, Lucia and Maria were as shocked by Antonia's appearance as her father was. Antonia had milky white skin and a tuft of frizzy, yellow hair on her head. She squinted during birth, betraying her light-sensitive pale blue eyes. When Lucia's doctor gave her an article about albinism the day after Antonia's birth, Lucia began to understand that albinism was a genetic condition, carried by both parents. But, it didn't matter to the baby's father. He wanted no part of raising a white child.

As Antonia grew, it became clear that she had trouble seeing. She started crying every time Lucia took her for a walk in her stroller, squinting and covering her eyes in the brutal Brazilian sunshine. At Antonia's first appointment for her vaccinations at the state-owned pediatric clinic, the harried doctor took one quick look at the baby and said, "You'd better put this child in a school for the blind. She is an albino and she will never be able to succeed in regular school."

This devastating opinion was the beginning of the end for Lucia. Although she was fiercely protective of her only child, she found it increasingly difficult to cope with the needs of a child who was legally blind and who couldn't tolerate the hot Brazilian sun. As if that wasn't enough stress, Lucia discovered that the government balked at granting social security benefits for Antonia's care. Although visual impairment was covered as a disability for all Brazilian citizens, the government argued that albinism was not a disability. Every individual with albinism was treated as an individual case in Brazil, and it took over a year of frequent meetings in downtown Salvador with government officials before Antonia was deemed eligible for benefits. Lucia's numerous absences from her job as a waitress to fight for Antonia's rights ultimately cost her that job.

Maria paused her recollections long enough to say "goodbye" when Jose left the house. He seemed like a nice boy, and Maria resisted the temptation to question Antonia about their relationship. Her granddaughter went into her bedroom, and Maria returned to her sewing and her memories.

Antonia was still a toddler when Lucia began staying out all night. Maria begged her to stay home with Antonia but Lucia was determined to escape the reminders of how difficult her life had become. Lucia was 23 years old when she was found dead in an alley in the worst part of Salvador, a needle still in her arm. Antonia was four years old.

Maria took on all the responsibilities of raising a child with albinism. She took Antonia to the pediatric clinic for consultations with eye and skin specialists and she met with school officials when Antonia was old enough to attend school. But those meetings did little to prevent the bullying and taunts that followed Antonia throughout her childhood. Maria couldn't count the number of times Antonia came home from school in tears or wailing, "Why do the other kids hate me?" Maria tried to help Antonia make friends in the neighborhood, only to find that other families were afraid that somehow her beautiful granddaughter would infect their children. Maria even made copies of the Albinism Fact Sheet that she had been given to her at the clinic and gave them to her neighbors. Nothing seemed to overcome the ignorance and misconceptions about albinism.

Now Antonia had made a friend—a black Brazilian boy who did not have albinism. While most of the people of Brazil have some combination of European, African and indigenous ancestry, the city of Salvador is 80% Black, the highest percentage in the country. Even though nine years of education are compulsory in Brazil, most of the children in Salvador stop attending school after primary school, especially in the poor neighborhoods like the one where Maria lived with Antonia. Despite her social isolation, Antonia loved school and was now in her last year of high school. She hoped to pass her entrance exams for university and train to be a nurse. Maria was proud of her granddaughter's academic achievements but what really astonished her was Antonia's determination in spite of her limitations.

I wish Lucia was here to see how her daughter has grown up so strong and self-assured, Maria thought to herself. *She would be so proud.* The thought of her daughter, gone now for twelve years, brought tears to her eyes.

Just then, Antonia walked into the room and said, "Avo, are you still sewing? You must be hungry and tired. Let me make you some chicken and rice soup. I know how to make it. I've been watching you and I can do it."

Maria smiled, got up, and gave her granddaughter a hug.

"What is that for?" Antonia asked.

"Oh nothing. Let's go into the kitchen. I want to watch you make my soup!"

Canada

| Charlotte and Oliver |

It was Teen Game Night at the Annual Conference of the National Organization of Albinism and Hypopigmentation (NOAH) in Tampa, Florida. Oliver had just taken a seat at a card table with a deck of large print playing cards when a girl came over to his table.

"Can I join you for a game of fish?"

"Sure," Oliver replied. "It's Charlotte right? I'm Oliver."

"Yeah, I can see your name badge. Well, if I squint hard enough, that is." Charlotte laughed an easy, almost musical laugh.

"You must have great eyesight if you can see my badge," she added.

"No, I remember you from our session this morning. You asked the speaker if she knew anything about accessibility for students with visual impairments at Memorial University in Newfoundland. I perked up because I am also Canadian and I'm also hoping to attend university next fall. I live in Toronto. Where do you live?"

"Vancouver." Charlotte smiled. Oliver smiled.

And the rest is history, as they say. They played cards for a couple of hours and talked late into the night. They attended the rest of the conference together and made plans to chat online with each other once a week after they both returned home.

Oliver has a mild form of oculocutaneous albinism with pale skin, light yellow hair, and dark blue eyes. His vision impairment is the only aspect of albinism that gives him difficulty. While he found that he didn't need a cane at his high school, Oliver uses a white cane to get around the busy streets of Toronto. The general public recognizes that a white cane means blindness, even if they don't realize that blindness exists on a wide spectrum. So when people see Oliver at an intersection with his cane, most know to offer help or stop their cars until he is safely on the other side.

Up until the day Oliver met Charlotte, his experience with dating was nil. In fact, he had little experience with friendship at all, regardless of gender. He learned the hard way that high school was all about fitting in. While Oliver's albinism was not as severe as some others at the NOAH conference, his need for magnifiers and other assistive technology made him a target for bullying at school. Girls seemed to pity him and other boys avoided him. Oliver suffered in silence and couldn't wait to graduate.

But everything changed after he met Charlotte. She understood him in a way that others couldn't. Charlotte also had oculocutaneous albinism, but her condition was more serious than his. She had white hair and light, almost translucent, eyes. Her vision impairment was also more severe than Oliver's. She used a white cane to get around everywhere. What impressed Oliver most about

Charlotte was her determination to live life to the fullest. When she told him that she skied almost every weekend during the winter, he was astonished.

Charlotte is a member of the British Columbia Blind Sports and Recreation Association, an organization that provides sighted ski guides and training to those with vision impairments. Charlotte's parents introduced her to adaptive skiing as a small child and now she competes in major national events. On Oliver's first trip to visit her in Vancouver, three months after the NOAH Conference, she took him to the ski resort to see what all her excitement was about. By the next year, they were skiing together and Oliver never looked back.

Charlotte and Oliver both decided to attend Memorial University in St. John's, Newfoundland, with Charlotte studying special education and Oliver studying ocean sciences. Their relationship evolved slowly online during their last year in high school and then quickly at university together. Like Oliver, Charlotte had no experience with dating. However, she was the more extraverted of the two, and she enjoyed meeting new people. Oliver, on the other hand, was awkward around others and preferred watching movies and playing chess. By the time they started university together, they had learned to utilize one another's strengths, and they were in love.

Walking around the campus hand-in-hand, they were a curiosity at first. Most of the other students had little experience with someone with albinism. More than once upon meeting another student for the first time, the couple was asked, "Are you brother and sister?" Charlotte would smile and learn over to give Oliver a quick kiss.

"Does that answer your question?" she would ask and then laugh with amusement at the reaction.

Like any couple, Charlotte and Oliver learned to support one another. Because Charlotte's vision was more impaired than Oliver's, they developed an unspoken language as they walked together. When Oliver noticed an obstacle in their path, he would give two quick squeezes of Charlotte's hand. They avoided many a student on the campus sidewalks and countless trees on their weekend hikes in St. John's parks that way. At university events and parties, Charlotte took the lead and initiated conversations with their fellow students. They were a team and they shared strategies to make life easier for two people with albinism.

Like many universities, Memorial University offered a variety of services to students with disabilities. Charlotte and Oliver availed themselves of these services even before arriving for their freshman year by communicating with the university's Centre for Students with Disabilities. Meetings with prospective faculty and registering for screen readers enabled them to be ready for their first day of class. Because of their vision impairments, both Charlotte and Oliver qualified for on-campus housing for their entire four-year program. This accommodation, more than any other, sold them on attending Memorial

University since neither of them had a driver's license.

Charlotte always knew that she wanted to be a teacher. Her positive experience with the ski guides, as well as the ways in which her teachers at university were always willing to help convinced her that special education would be a perfect fit. Oliver's program in ocean sciences enabled him to combine his math and science bent with a passion for ocean conservation. After graduating from university, the couple decided to stay in St. John's. Oliver was accepted into the university's graduate program in ocean sciences and Charlotte got a special education teacher's position in the St. John's school system.

Happily, the couple graduated with a surprise announcement for their family and friends. Charlotte and Oliver planned a winter wedding – on top of a mountain at the Vancouver ski resort they both loved. The January wedding made national news in Canada as the couple had become a celebrity of sorts for their inspiring love story and their success in overcoming their mutual visual limitations.

At the conclusion of the ceremony on top of the ski slope, Charlotte handed her flowers to her mother and put on her skis. She turned to her long-time ski guide and with a grin, asked her, "Are you ready?"

"Yes, let's do this!" the guide replied.

The guide stepped off the platform onto the ski slope, quickly followed by Charlotte. Twenty seconds later, Oliver turned to his guide and said, "Let's go get my bride!" Following closely behind his guide, Oliver descended the slope, whooping with glee the entire way. Everyone on the platform clapped and cheered. It was perfect.

China

| Chang |

The street lights shone through the gathering evening mist as Chang walked along a major shopping boulevard in his city of Chongqing, China. It was about 7:00 at night and most of the shops were closed. However, restaurants were still open and the nighttime crowd of 20-somethings were replacing the shoppers and workers that normally filled the street. Chang spent most of this evenings on this street, finding his dinner in one of the more than 30,000 hot pot restaurants that Chongqing was famous for.

Chang sat down at a sidewalk café and ordered a vegetable hot pot to have with his beer. Within ten minutes, the waiter brought a steaming pot of broth to his table. Various ingredients were placed around the pot, including raw vegetables, tofu, dumplings, and noodles. The meal was delicious and Chang made a mental note to eat here again in the future. Tonight he ate quickly, glancing at his phone frequently. He did not want to be late for his weekly singles group meeting two blocks away.

For the last two years, Chang had been attending this group in hopes of making friends, and perhaps even finding a wife. It had taken him a long time to get up the courage to attend his first group meeting. Chang has albinism and his white hair and pale skin make him stand out in any group of Chinese people. He anticipated the stares he would receive upon arriving for his first

19

meeting of the singles group. But now, two years later, he no longer cares whenever a new member arrives at a meeting and gives him the inevitable startled look.

The singles group is really a forum for unmarried Chinese men and women to meet each other in a speed dating format. A typical two-hour meeting consists of the 10 to12 members rotating among each other for timed, informal conversations. Time is set aside at the end of each meeting to share experiences from their conversations or anything from their lives that would be helpful to others in the group. Chang's conversations consist primarily of answering his partner's questions about his albinism. Consequently, Chang quickly realized that most of his partners were not really interested in him. It was discouraging to Chang but he keeps attending the meetings. He doesn't have other friends and the weekly meetings are his only opportunity to have contact with people his own age.

In China, albinism is not well understood. The genetic condition traditionally has been considered bad luck, leaving people with albinism ostracized and excluded from mainstream society. In a culture where fitting in is highly prized, many babies with albinism are given up for adoption. And those children that are not rejected by their families are frequently denied educational opportunities and good jobs.

Chang grew up on a farm several hundred miles west of Chongqing. During his childhood, he stayed home to work with his father in the fields while his two older sisters went to school. When his mother died and his father remarried, his new stepmother insisted he leave home and find work in the city. At eighteen, Chang moved to Chongqing, where he found a job loading boxes at a clothing factory. He was shunned by most of his coworkers so he spent his off-hours learning to read and write at a local adult education center. The government of China doesn't recognize albinism as a disability so Chang wasn't given any special assistance for his poor vision— not even eyeglasses. But he eventually saved enough money to purchase his first pair of glasses. After a couple of years, Chang was promoted to a factory supervisor job. For the first time, Chang felt like he might be able to lead a satisfying, if not a happy, life.

Chang walked into tonight's singles group meeting just a few minutes early. He took one of the remaining two chairs at the back of the room but glanced up to see one more person walk into the room. The young woman with long white hair and pale skin, looked anxious as everyone, including Chang, turned and stared at her. She hurried over to the last chair that was next to Chang and sat down. Her cheeks were red as she looked down at her lap.

At that same moment, another male group member spoke up. "Look everyone! Chang's twin has joined us!"

Before he could think, Chang jumped up and responded, "She is not my twin. She obviously has albinism though, as I do. I think we should show her respect and welcome her to the group."

Chang sat down again, wondering what had gotten into him, challenging the status quo that way. The leader would surely not appreciate it and perhaps even kick both men out of the group. He glanced at the woman seated next to him who was now staring at him and smiling.

"Thank you," she whispered.

The group leader did not kick out either Chang or the man who made the rude comment. Inexplicably, the leader ignored the exchange between the two. He seemed to pretend it never happened. Neither did he welcome the new young woman to the group. Chang thought that was probably too much to expect. In China, people with albinism are considered to be inferior—both physically and mentally. Maybe the leader ignored the two of them, hoping they would just quit the group.

When the speed dating began, Chang turned to the young woman and asked, "Who would have thought there would be two of us in this group? What is your name?"

"I am Mingzhu. What is yours?"

"Chang. You have a beautiful name, Mingzhu."

Mingzhu blushed and Chang wondered if he had been too forward. But they started talking and when the timer went off, signaling a change in conversation partners, Mingzhu did not move. Chang was ecstatic. At the end of the meeting, he asked Mingzhu if she would like to meet him for dinner on the shopping boulevard before next week's meeting. She said yes.

Mingzhu's background was quite different from that

of Chang. However, her experience trying to fit into China's mainstream society was just as complicated. Mingzhu lived the first year of her life in an orphanage, with very little love or stimulation. In fact, when the British couple who eventually adopted her first met her, she was malnourished and not even crawling, much less walking. But Mingzhu became one of the lucky ones, adopted into a family who loved and nurtured her. Her father was a construction engineer who consulted with many companies for China's booming urban construction industry. Her mother stayed at home with Mingzhu, making sure her daughter had help with her vision impairment and that she had protection from the sun. Because the family moved from city to city, Mingzhu never made long-lasting friends. She was homeschooled and then earned her college degree online. When she was 23, her father retired from his job. He and Mingzhu's mother decided to return to London while Mingzhu resolved to remain in her homeland.

Mingzhu had a good human resources job in an international company in Chongqing that once employed her father. But she had few friends other than those she met online. When she decided to join the singles group, she considered it her final effort to create an independent life for herself in China. If she wasn't successful finding friends in this group, she would join her parents in London.

Chang was so eager to see Mingzhu again that he counted the hours until they met for dinner the following week before their singles group meeting. They shared a hot pot dinner at the same café he had found the previous week and they talked about their hopes and dreams. They laughed together when passersby stared at them and they answered nondefensively when their waiter asked innocently, "Are you two twins?"

Despite their vastly different upbringings, they connected in a way that only those with a common condition, such as albinism, can. Within six months, they were planning to marry. While their wedding was a small event, everyone from their singles group attended. It was the happiest day of Chang and Mingzhu's life.

The couple continued to live in Chongqing and their notoriety grew. It wasn't long before the city newspaper published a story about the "married albinos" who defied Chinese stereotypes about their lives. Their ability to live independent, productive lives was fascinating to many Chinese citizens. Chang and Mingzhu evolved into role models for anyone who felt different from the norms of Chinese society. They gave talks at local schools and clubs, striving to encourage anyone who felt alone or isolated.

Five years later, with one child who had albinism and another baby on the way, Chang and Mingzhu decided to join a new group—the Chinese Organization for Albinism (COA). Emboldened by the positive response they received from other groups, they eagerly accepted leadership roles in the COA. Chang and Mingzhu knew it was time to help bring about hope for a normal life to others with albinism in China.

Guna Yala Islands, Panama

| Yaixa |

The Guna people, (often called Kuna) one of Panama's seven indigenous groups, have a population of 60,000 (one in seven of whom are carriers of the albinism gene) and are natives of an archipelago of small islands in the Caribbean waters off Panama. Many of the islets are more than five hours by boat from the coast and even the most heavily populated have no more than 1,000 inhabitants.

Although half of the population lives in Panama City, they continue to marry other Guna from their home islands.

I sat with my mama at our stall on the plaza, selling crafts to the tourists. I went to the stall after school a couple of days a week, but it never felt like work. I loved spending time with Mama, who was always in a good mood and loved to tell stories. Today, she was beginning to tell me the story of the molas, the colorful, embroidered fabric squares that we, and many women in Guna Yala, sold in our stall. Before she could finish the story, however, a family—mother, father, one daughter and one young son— came up to us. A cruise ship had just arrived at the dock two blocks away and many of the passengers walked eagerly toward the shopping plaza of our village.

"Welcome," Mama said with a friendly smile as she jumped up from her chair. "We have lots of beautiful molas and pottery made by the women in our village."

As the tourists looked at the molas on display in our stall, I thought about the women of our village who made them. They were mostly the mothers and grandmothers of my friends, and they worked long, hard hours on the layers of cotton and intricate borders that made up these cheerful squares of fabric. These village women would usually meet in small groups, sewing by hand and sharing the latest news of the village. Recently, Mama had started to teach me some of the more simple designs.

"Yes, these are beautiful. Do you have any blouses or skirts made of these squares?" the woman asked.

"No," Mama responded. "These molas are part of our cultural heritage and we don't want others wearing our traditional costumes. But the fabric squares can be made into many things, such as placemats or pillow cases. Or they can be framed into art for your wall."

"I love the idea of framing them," the woman exclaimed. Before she could say anything else, her son pointed at me and looked up at his mother.

"Mommy, why is that girl so white?"

His mother, embarrassed, tried to hush her son, but

his curiosity wasn't stifled. He spoke even louder, "But Mommy, tell me why she looks like that. Is she sick?"

"No, son. She isn't sick."

She glanced frantically at her husband and then continued speaking to her son. "Why don't you, your sister, and your dad take a walk to see the other stalls and what they are selling? Look for someplace to get ice cream."

As the rest of her family strolled off, the mother smiled apologetically at Mama and said, "I'm so sorry for my son's comments. Please forgive us."

But Mama just smiled at the embarrassed woman and said. "Don't apologize for your son. He is just curious. My beautiful daughter," she said as she pulled me toward her, "has albinism, which is not unusual in our village. Her doctor told me there is one person with albinism born for every 145 Kuna Indian births. We believe people with albinism are very special and it is a blessing for a family to have such a child. These children are referred to as Sipus, and they have the duty of defending the Moon against a dragon who tries to devour it during lunar eclipses. They are given special bows and arrows to shoot down the dragon and they are the only ones allowed to be out on the nights of these eclipses."

Mama went on to explain that our family has other sipus—an uncle and two cousins. She said that while she loves me, it is hard to afford the medical care that I required. I listened to Mama describe my poor eyesight and how I must see my eye doctor every six months.

27

"Yaixa is only six years old and already has the skin lesions that plague so many of our sipus," Mama explained. "It is hard to keep her out of the sun even though I've tried to explain the dangers to her. Sometimes I am sad that Yaixa can't enjoy her childhood like her friends. We take her out to the beach in the evenings when the sun sets. It is beautiful then but she misses her friends from the village who don't have to worry about the sun."

While Mama talked to the mother, I tried to inch away from them and hide behind a chair. When the boy first pointed at me, it didn't bother me so much. I was used to people staring and sometimes even pointing at me. But the more Mama talked, the more upset I became.

I wasn't sure why, but I felt my eyes become teary and I wiped them with my dress. Maybe I was upset because I began to think about my Uncle Carlos, who was very sick. He spent the days indoors in his hut, only occasionally going to sit on his patio after the sun went down. My aunt took care of the many sores on his skin and took him to medical appointments. Whenever I visited him, he always seemed so sad. For the first time, I began to wonder about my own future—would I be sick and sad like Uncle Carlos?

After the woman purchased several molas and left, Mama went back to her chair in the stall. She pulled me onto her lap and asked me why I was crying. After I shared my fears about whether my life would be like that of Uncle Carlos, Mama drew me close. Her strong arms gave me comfort and her words were soothing.

"Yaixa, I am going to sing a song to you. I know you're not a baby anymore but no one can see us so just listen." She continued to hug me and began to sing softly.

"I was born in Guna Yala
I used to play in my homeland
I grew up in the middle of the sea
I was born surrounded by coconut trees
Our moms spent their days sewing winis and molas
Our fathers went to work in the fields everyday
Our grandparents offered up their prayers to Babummad..."

It was a song I had heard Mama sing as long as I could remember, but today it had a different effect on me. Instead of just helping me drift off to sleep at bedtime, it made me feel strong knowing that I was part of a wonderful culture, community, and family. Mama couldn't guarantee my future but she could guarantee my identity—a loved, special member of a strong Guna society. I would never be alone, and together we would conquer anything I might face.

Hong Kong

| Mei-Zhen |

Mei-Zhen was seven years old when she realized that she was different from the other girls at school. It was Picture Day at her school and Mei-Zhen spent days planning what to wear. She carefully considered all the dresses in her closet, trying on several for her grandmother, Waipo, who perched on Mei-Zhen's bed, clapping in delight every time Mei-Zhen pirouetted in front of her in a different dress. The dress that Mei-Zhen finally chose was a chintz, empire waist dress that her mother had given her for her last birthday. It was white with large pink flowers. The long sleeves ended with gathered lace at the wrists, as well as on the high neckline.

On the morning of Picture Day, Mei-Zhen chattered with excitement as Waipo walked her to school. They took their usual path, past other high-rise apartment buildings, shops, and markets. Shopowners were sweeping the sidewalks in front of their establishments and some smiled and waved at the little girl and her grandmother. Mei-Zhen could hardly contain her excitement at wearing her beautiful dress to school. She skipped ahead of Waipo, stopping to say "Good morning" to the familiar old women selling tea and toast at their food stalls along the route.

Mei-Zhen attended a private, international school in Hong Kong, a school noted for its excellent reputation, as well as its high tuition costs. Its close proximity to the high-rise apartment building where Mei-Zhen lived with her parents and Waipo provided day-to-day routine and familiarity which the family valued. Mei-Zhen's parents both worked in international banking. They left for work early every morning and sometimes didn't return until after Mei-Zhen was in bed for the night. Like many other Chinese families, Waipo lived with her daughter's family, assuming virtually all child care responsibilities for Mei-Zhen. She made sure that Mei-Zhen felt loved and safe—they rarely ventured into the city beyond the area immediately surrounding their building. Waipo knew that strangers' stares and gestures would surely be directed at the little girl with the white hair and pale skin.

When Mei-Zhen entered her classroom that morning, seven years of her family's efforts to protect her from the real world's cruelty disappeared in a flash. Instead of smiling and complimenting Mei-Zhen on her beautiful dress, two of her classmates pointed at her and giggled. Others glanced at her and then looked away. Confused, Mei-Zhen sat down at her desk and looked around. While none of the other girls wore their usual school uniform, Mei-Zhen noticed that the other girls' outfits were different from hers in style and cut. Most of the dresses were simple jumpers with short-sleeve blouses. A few girls wore skirts with u-neck tops, simple necklaces visible on their open neckline. Mei-Zhen looked down at her flowery dress and suddenly wished she was invisible.

While her long sleeves and high neckline protected her fair skin from the hot September sun, it also emphasized her differences from the other girls.

Why did I wear this ugly dress? Mei-Zhen thought to herself as she lined up with her classmates for their sessions with the photographer. When it came time for her to sit on the stool in front of the black photographer's drape, Mei-Zhen was near tears. The photographer, a patient woman who had photographed wiggly children for years, was stopped in her tracks by the vision in front of her. There sat Mei-Zhen, her long white hair framing her delicate face, looking down at her lap.

"Why do you look so sad?" The photographer asked in a low, kindly voice as she walked over to Mei-Zhen. She lifted up the little girl's chin and stared at the china-blue eyes framed by white lashes.

"Why, you are the most beautiful little girl I've seen all day! And you picked the perfect dress for such an important event as your school portrait!"

A little smile began to emerge on Mei-Zhen's face and she sat up a little straighter.

Encouraged by her success, the photographer went on. "I bet you're going to grow up to be a famous model or fashion designer. Will you promise to visit me in fifteen years, after you grow up? I'll be right here, looking for another little girl as beautiful as you!"

Later, at the end of the school day, Waipo met her granddaughter at the school's gate and asked Mei-Zhen the same questions she asked every day. "How was your day? Did you learn something new?"

Mei-Zen, who had already begun to skip ahead, turned to Waipo and replied, "I'm going to be a famous model someday!"

The years flew by and every day Mei-Zhen walked to school with her beloved Waipo. She began to understand that she was physically different from the other girls in her school but she always remembered the photographer's words. She was beautiful and her differences made her more interesting to people. She made friends easily and she did well in school. She still encountered stares and giggles from new students and strangers, but Mei-Zhen just responded with her sweet smile. She learned as much as she could about albinism and how important it was to protect her skin. One of her favorite things to do was shop for unique clothing which she modeled for her grandmother. She began to wear some of her unusual outfits to school on days when their uniforms weren't required. Instead of hiding her differences from others, Mei-Zhen embraced her differences as part of her unique and memorable style.

When she was fifteen, Mei-Zhen accompanied her parents on a summer trip to Paris. It was a revelation to the teenager. As she walked the city streets, she was astounded by how different EVERYONE was! White, black, brown, and every hue of skin tone in-between. But what was even more interesting to Mei-Zhen was the variety of dress.

33

Mei-Zhen drank in the shapes, colors, and textures of the costumes she saw on the women everywhere she went. By the end of their trip, Mei-Zhen knew that she had to return and be part of this vibrant city.

For the next three years, Mei-Zhen explored the world of fashion design. Her parents bought her a sewing machine and she began designing outfits. By the time she was accepted at a renowned school of fashion in Paris, she had a small portfolio and several videos of herself modeling her own creations. Waipo was always her first and most appreciative audience, and Mei-Zhen practiced modeling in her family's living room to gain self-confidence. She also sent copies of her video to Diandra Forrest, the first African-American model with albinism to be signed to a major modeling agency.

Diandra immediately offered to mentor Mei-Zhen after she arrived in Paris and introduce her to the world of modeling. Two years after starting fashion school, Mei-Zhen accepted a modeling contract with a famous designer based in Paris to model in his haute couture show. When the day of the show arrived, Mei-Zhen entered the models' dressing room and found two of the other models staring at her and giggling. Her memories of that painful day thirteen years earlier when she first realized how others reacted to her came flooding back. This time, Mei-Zhen walked over to the two models, smiled, and said, "Don't worry, ladies. I wasn't offered this gig because I have albinism. I was hired because I look good in these clothes. Besides, isn't being different why we're all here? I don't know a single model who looks like the girls who buy these clothes."

A few years later, on a trip back home to Hong Kong to see her family, Mei-Zhen found out that Picture Day was scheduled that week at her old school. Walking up the stairs into the school with Waipo, who was by now a bit slower but no less supportive of her granddaughter, Mei-Zhen walked past a couple of young girls. Neither of them giggled but they did stare. One of them rushed up to Mei-Zhen and exclaimed, "Aren't you Mei-Zhen, the famous model? I collect all your pictures!"

Mei-Zhen smiled her sweet smile and headed for the room where a patient woman taking photos was helping another young girl to relax. Mei-Zhen couldn't wait to thank the photographer for the words that helped her to make her dreams come true.

India

| Vivaan |

As Vivaan practiced with his football team members on the field after school on that hot September afternoon, he wondered if his little brother, Aditya, would be okay walking home alone when his primary school classes ended for the day. The football season required after-class practice three days a week and Vivaan's two sisters usually accompanied Aditya safely home when Vivaan was at practice. But today, the girls were on an extended day field trip so Aditya would have to walk the five blocks home by himself.

Vivaan's anxiety increased as he wondered, *Did Aditya remember his hat and his sunglasses? If he didn't, he won't be able to see well in the hot sun. What if other kids make fun of him? Would Aditya ignore any taunts?* For a moment, Vivaan wondered if he should leave practice to make sure his brother was okay. But he stopped himself by considering how he had learned to take care of himself when he was seven years old, the same age Aditya was now. Vivaan turned his attention back to the coach and sighed. The two brothers both had albinism and Vivaan knew life would never be easy for his little brother, just as it continued to be rough for himself. At some point though, Aditya wouldn't have his big brother to take care of him.

Ever since his siblings were born, Vivaan knew it was his duty, as firstborn, to look after them all. But, Vivaan felt a special obligation toward Aditya. The girls would look out for each other, Vivaan reasoned, but Aditya needed him. Nobody else in their immediate family had albinism except their maternal grandmother, Nani. Vivaan always admired Nani, who managed to raise three children alone after her husband was killed in a car accident. Despite her poor vision, Nani took in sewing and laundry from neighbors and made sure her children were well-fed and well-educated. The same villagers who paid Nani for her services shunned her in public, but she didn't seem to mind. She once told Vivaan that "Cruelty comes from ignorance. Show them your wisdom."

When Vivaan was born, Nani stepped in to help with his care, making sure to dress her grandson in protective clothing and sunglasses whenever he was outside, a precaution Vivaan appreciated only many years later. Vivaan's parents were aware that having a child with albinism was a genetic possibility, but when they saw his white hair and translucent skin for the first time, their shock was quickly followed by anxiety. How could they raise a child that looked so different in a country like India? Only Nani's strength and unconditional acceptance of her first grandson enabled Vivaan's parents to move beyond their fears. It wasn't long before they began to love their new baby with a fierceness they never imagined. With Nani's guidance, they began preparing their son to thrive in a country where persistent ignorance of albinism creates fewer economic opportunities, social stigma, and emotional anguish.

Vivaan did thrive. But it was never easy. His family diligently took him to ophthalmologists and dermatologists for regular examinations. His eyesight could not be corrected completely by glasses and he suffered from light sensitivity, rapid eye movements, and misaligned eyes. When one ophthalmologist suggested that Vivaan should be enrolled in a private school for the blind, his parents bristled. "No, our son is not blind and he will not live away from his family until he chooses to."

Indian culture has traditionally valued fair shades of brown skin color. Ironically, that value does not extend to the total lack of skin and hair melanin that is characteristically part of albinism. Vivaan felt the sting of name-calling from an early age. Children yelled insults, such as "ghost," and "whitey." Many people didn't believe he was Indian, calling him "foreigner." Once, when he tried to cross the border with his family back into India from Pakistan, the government official didn't believe his passport.

Vivaan learned to ignore the stares of strangers and let the taunts roll off his back by sharing his feelings with his family. These family discussions became a regular part of life as Vivaan grew older. While Vivaan's parents emphasized their unconditional love for their son, they also focused on educating his sisters about the causes and symptoms of albinism and how to respond to others' ignorance. As a result, Vivaan's sisters helped him handle the schoolyard bullies more effectively. They stood up to them and took every opportunity to share the facts about albinism with their friends and neighbors. Over time, Vivaan grew into an active boy who looked different but was not considered "less than."

Now that Aditya was in school, the family turned its attention to helping him cope with albinism and the inevitable challenges he would face from Indian society. Aditya's first day in the village's primary school was a new beginning, not only for the young boy, but also for his family. It signaled a transition from Aditya's safety and acceptance in his family home to the unknowns he would encounter in school.

Vivaan and his parents visited with Aditya's new teacher and prepared her for the physical assistance he needed to succeed with his schoolwork, as well as how to deal with possible harassment from other children. Having Vivaan present helped the young teacher to understand what albinism really is and what it isn't, not what she had seen in movies or heard from ignorant colleagues. Vivaan's robust health and self-confidence embodied the hopes and dreams that his family had for Aditya. Vivaan made sure to share his own challenges trying to fit into traditional Indian culture. He knew that his little brother might have even greater difficulties.

Aditya's vision was worse than Vivaan's poor eyesight. With eyeglasses and a front row seat in his classrooms, Vivaan was able to succeed in his studies. In fact, he was so successful that now, at age 15 and in his first year of secondary school, Vivaan was beginning to consider university. As the first person in his family to potentially attend university, his family was extremely proud of their son's achievements.

Aditya's even greater challenges with albinism could make it more difficult for him to be as successful as his brother. While Vivaan's eyes were a pale blue, Aditya's eyes were pink, evidence of his more severe vision limitations. To help him read and see the blackboard, Aditya's backpack included special magnifying glasses and sunglasses. Aditya's extreme sensitivity to sunlight made it difficult for him to play outside. In consultation with school officials, his family requested that accommodations be made to include Aditya as much as possible in team sports and outside games. His family, always prepared with ideas, suggested that shade umbrellas be available outside and that Aditya be offered roles such as time-keeper or even assistant coach. These accommodations allowed Aditya to stand under the umbrella during class recess activities outside and still feel part of the activities.

That hot afternoon on the football practice field, Vivaan reflected on his family's expectations and the assistance that Aditya required. *I pray to Lord Shiva that Aditya made it home safely,* Vivaan thought. *But what if he couldn't see well enough and took a wrong turn? Or what if someone taunted him and made him cry? I could never forgive myself if anything happened to my little brother.*

When practice ended for the day, Vivaan raced over

to the primary school, located just across the street. He made sure that Aditya did leave the classroom and that he was seen beginning to walk home. As Vivaan briskly walked the dusty village streets, he pulled down his baseball cap to shade his eyes from the still bright afternoon sun. He looked left and right, trying to see any unusual activity or individuals. When he had walked a couple of blocks, he caught a glimpse of something—or someone—to his left, crouched down against the side of the village bakery shop.

Vivaan turned and walked over to not one, but two small figures. His heart jumped when he realized that it was Aditya. And next to him was a small, white puppy, obviously happy, getting his belly scratched.

"What are you doing, Aditya?" yelled Vivaan. "I was so worried about you."

"Look Vivaan, this puppy is just like me!" Aditya replied with a calm smile.

And sure enough, the puppy had white fur and pink eyes—*an albino, for sure,* Vivaan realized. The puppy was scrawny, dirty, and apparently alone, as no other dogs were nearby.

"I was trying to get away from some boys after they grabbed my hat and sunglasses," Aditya continued. "I was running and trying to shade my eyes but I didn't see the wall of the bakery. I ran into the wall and scraped my knee. I sat down and this puppy came up to me and tried to lick my knee."

Aditya grabbed the puppy and held him close. "Lord Shiva sent him to me. Can I keep him, please?"

Vivaan was too occupied looking around for the boys who had stolen his brother's hat and sunglasses to hear Aditya's pleas. He alternated between feeling fury at the bullies and relief that Aditya wasn't hurt badly. He also felt shame for letting his little brother walk home alone. He decided then and there that he would take care of Aditya for the rest of his life.

Using his long shirt sleeve, Vivaan wiped off the dirt and blood from Aditya's scraped knee. He gave him his hat and sunglasses to wear during the rest of the walk home. Aditya picked up the puppy and again turned to his older brother.

"Will Mata and Pita let me keep him? I want to call him *Upahara* because he is a gift from Lord Shiva." He hugged the puppy, who responded with a furious tail wag.

And so it was that many lessons were learned that day. Vivaan learned the value of family responsibility. Aditya learned the importance of compassion; and the street bullies learned (a few days later) never to underestimate the family with albinism who lived in their village.

Israel

| Hiba |

Hiba arrived at 9:00 am that Monday for her summer internship at the Michaelson Institute for Rehabilitation of Vision at Hadassah University Medical Center in Jerusalem. She had been working since her high school graduation at the highly-regarded facility that enables children as young as two months to capitalize on whatever vision they have. One month watching miracles unfold was all it took for Hiba to make a life-changing decision. She decided she wanted a career in medicine.

"Hi Rachel." Hiba smiled, greeting the nurse supervisor on the post-op floor where she would spend the next week of her summer internship. Hiba's internship was structured to introduce her to many of the departments and functions of the Institute. Over the last month, she had worked in Medical Records, Human Resources, and Registration. Hiba liked them all but she was fascinated with Human Resources, maybe because of the people skills she saw demonstrated. Hiba had always been a people person, and now she wondered if nursing or other aspects of patient care might be in her future.

"Good morning, Hiba," Rachel replied.

They had met the previous week in Human Resources, while Hiba was completing some paperwork required for her to work in patient care areas of the Institute. Rachel noticed then that Hiba had albinism but didn't seem to have impaired vision, other than needing eyeglasses.

Rachel closed her computer program and asked Hiba if she'd like to join her for a cup of tea in the hospital cafeteria. She wanted to get to know Hiba and how she could best support her during her week on the post-op floor. As they walked toward the cafeteria, Rachel noticed how naturally Hiba smiled and said "hello" to everyone she passed.

They found a small table in the corner of the large cafeteria where the noise was at a slightly lower decibel.

"Are you ready to learn all about what we do on the post-op wing?" Rachel asked.

"Oh yes. I'm really excited to see how patients, especially children, are cared for. I have memories of when I had my eye surgery here when I was about four years old so it means a lot to me that I'm back as a student."

This was the opening Rachel was hoping for. "So, Hiba, what kind of surgery did you have here?"

"I had my nystagmus corrected here. Now I have almost perfect vision as long as I wear my glasses. Oh, and of course I have to wear sunglasses outside."

"You're really fortunate that your albinism didn't affect your eyes very much. We treat a lot of children with albinism here who have very impaired vision. Tell me about yourself. I saw from your bio that your parents are from Sudan."

Hiba put her teacup down and looked at Rachel. Rachel thought she saw a touch of sadness in her eyes.

"Well, it's kind of a long story. I was born in Israel but my family used to live in Sudan. My grandfather was Jewish and my grandmother was Sudanese. They lived in the Jewish community in South Sudan. That's where my father was born. That's why my last name is Cohen."

Rachel interrupted. "I thought that all the Jews left Sudan in the 1960s due to anti-Semitic attacks."

"Most of the Jewish people left in the late 1960s and emigrated to the UK, Greece, the USA, and Israel. That included my grandparents and my father, who was still a boy then. They moved to Greece for about 15 years. When my grandmother got cancer, they came back to Sudan at her request. She died in her homeland about two years later, but not before my dad fell in love with a Sudanese girl. My Mom and Dad were married in Sudan and tried to find work—my Dad ended up getting a job as an electrician in Khartoum. But life was still very hard for Jews in Sudan, even though both of my parents were born in Sudan. When my Mom got pregnant with me, they decided to come to Israel."

"As I'm sure you know, Israel's immigration policy is very strict, especially toward Africans. How were you and your family able to stay in this country?" Rachel asked.

"It is incredible, really," Hiba replied. "Africans with albinism are in great danger, especially in Tanzania, Malawi, Sudan, and some other countries. Because of the superstition that body parts from people with albinism will bring good luck, hundreds of people with albinism have been murdered or maimed, including children. There are many awful stories on the internet about these murders."

Hiba took a sip of her tea and continued. "My parents applied for political asylum in Israel because they were afraid that I would fall victim to the body-part traders in Sudan. They knew we could never go back to Sudan or any other African state. After about a year of investigating, the government approved their application for political asylum. And not only that. For the first time in Israel's history, the approval extended to my parents and my grandfather. We are truly grateful and my family has a great life here. My father got his master's degree in electrical engineering and he now works for Microsoft. My mother finished her college program and she works for Israel's Magen David Adom Society, Israel's counterpart to The Red Cross."

"My goodness, Hiba. That is quite a story. I can see why you feel so fortunate," Rachel said.

"Ironically, my albinism has helped me to fit in here in Israel. I am African but I don't feel the suspicion or hostility that other African refugees feel here. I really hope the day comes when other Africans—those who are just looking for a better life—will also be given asylum. I hope you don't mind me sharing my feelings about that," Hiba said.

Rachel was impressed by the maturity and self-confidence she experienced from this African-Israeli girl who had overcome so much. She knew what Hiba was hinting at. Anti-African sentiment, especially toward the thousands of Sudanese migrants, was rampant in Israel.

Those Israelis who felt that the Africans migrants were a threat to the Jewish character of their country called them infiltrators, a derogatory term adopted by President Netanyahu himself. Over the last decade, huge migrant camps had been built in the Israeli desert, holding African migrants in squalid conditions until they could be returned to their African homelands. Rachel felt it was indeed ironic that a Sudanese family that included a child with albinism would be embraced in Israel, whereas so many other migrants from Sudan would be denied any rights at all. The irony extended to how easily Hiba blended into her Israeli life. She was actually accepted because of her albinism, rather than shunned, as so many people with albinism were around the world. *Apparently*, Rachel mused, *being an albino was preferable to being Black.*

"No, Hiba. On the contrary, I admire your determination and positivity. I don't think you and I are going to solve the complicated issues you've raised and I have to get back to the post-op floor. But I've really enjoyed getting to know you and hearing your remarkable story. Let's go upstairs together. I think you should spend your first day with us tagging along with the shift nurses, getting familiar with everything we do. How does that sound?"

Hiba replied with a big smile. "Yes, I'm excited to be here. Let's get started!"

South Africa

| Enzokuhle |

Enzokuhle sat outside her home, playing in the dirt. She hoped for any semblance of a breeze to counteract the sweltering Soweto summer heat. It was still early morning but her face was covered with sweat and flies buzzed around her. She knew that she would have to move soon to avoid the sun beating down on her pale skin, but for now, she was interested in a group of beetles that were congregating next to her in the dirt.

I wonder if these beetles are a family, Enzokuhle thought to herself. *Which one is the mommy and which one is the daddy? Maybe this one, with the yellow spot, is the mommy because she is the prettiest.*

Enzokuhle's mother was inside their home, making bread. It was a stretch to call where they lived a home; it was really a shanty thrown together with sheets of corrugated metal, cardboard, and the occasional piece of wood. There were three of these shacks in the backyard of a cement block house and each was occupied by a family who paid rent to the owner of the house. This arrangement had become widespread as the housing crisis for poor black families living in Soweto reached epidemic proportions.

Enzokuhle's home had no electricity or running water, but at least it kept the sun out. She and the oldest of the four siblings, Junior, had albinism and were in constant danger of developing skin lesions that would become cancerous. Enzokuhle was the youngest of the four children and she had just turned five the previous month. Her mother, who had emigrated from Tanzania as a teenager, worked at a local restaurant washing dishes. Her father did odd jobs as he could find them. Recently, he had found a job doing yard work for a wealthy white family in the northern suburbs of Johannesburg and he came home only on the weekends.

Because Enzokuhle was not yet old enough to attend school, she usually accompanied her mother to her job in the restaurant. The restaurant, a loud and popular bistro near the Soweto Hotel and Conference Center, was a source of endless fascination for the little girl. The restaurant manager, a friendly black man with a gold tooth, gave her juice and cookies and let her sit on a stool just outside the door to the kitchen. He understood her mother's child care dilemma. As long as Enzokuhle didn't get in the way of the waitstaff or bother the customers, he accommodated her daughter's presence during her work shift. Enzokuhle sat quietly on her stool, with her little dolly on her lap, watching the customers who laughed, talked, and drank a lot. Sometimes, Enzokuhle would pretend she was one of them and she would hold her cup of juice *just so*. Then she would talk to her dolly, trying to sound as happy and grown-up as the customers.

"How are you Dolly? Are you going to order a drink? Yes, I like my juice very much, thank you," Enzokuhle said in a low voice to the doll in her lap.

49

Customers rarely spoke to Enzokuhle. This didn't surprise the little girl as she felt invisible to most people, other than her mother. When she walked to the market with her mother on Saturdays, her neighbors would wave and speak to her mother, but rarely to her. Recently, Enzokuhle began talking to Dolly on these trips; it made her feel less lonely.

One evening at the restaurant, Enzokuhle noticed one of the customers, a lady, smiling at her. She was sitting at a nearby table with a little girl about Enzokuhle's age seated next to her. Enzokuhle met her eyes and then quickly looked down at Dolly in her lap. She didn't want the manager to scold her for bothering the customers. But the look was enough to reveal to Enzokuhle that the lady looked just like her. She was a black lady who had white skin and yellow hair.

Albinism is not unusual among Blacks in South Africa but the only other black person that Enzokuhle knew who looked like her was her older brother, Junior. She didn't have any friends, and her mother always warned her to stay away from people she didn't know.

Within a few seconds the lady with albinism got up and walked over to Enzokuhle, her little girl in tow.

"Hello, what's your name?" the woman asked with a smile.

Enzokuhle was afraid to speak but the woman spoke again. "It's okay. You don't need to be afraid. My name is Lesedi and my daughter's name is Amahle."

Enzokuhle was scared. *Would this woman try to grab her and run off with her?*

Lesedi spoke again. "Is your mother or father here? I'd like to meet them. Maybe you and Amahle could play together sometime."

Enzokuhle looked up at Amahle's smiling face. *Amahle didn't have albinism like her mother. She looked like the other Blacks in Soweto. She seemed friendly and it would be nice to have a friend.*

After the two mothers met, they made plans to get together with their daughters. The next weekend, the four of them went to the market together. Enzokuhle didn't know what to talk about with Amahle, but Amahle didn't seem to mind. She kept up a constant stream of chatter. "What's your doll's name? I have a dog who licks me all the time. Do you like milk tarts? They're my favorite. What's your favorite color? Mine is yellow."

Amahle's friendliness soon put Enzokuhle at ease and the two little girls skipped, jumped puddles and waved at all the stall vendors. Amazingly for Enzokuhle, it was really fun!

That chance encounter began a lifelong friendship between Enzokuhle and Amahle, as well as between their families. Lesedi was a public health nurse who worked with poor families in Soweto. She helped Enzokuhle's mother get the sunscreen ointments and visual assistance tools that Enzokuhle needed to cope with her own albinism. Because Lesedi also had albinism, she often did training

51

for families who had children with the same condition. With her help, Enzokuhle and Junior developed better self-esteem and learned how to stand up to bullies.

But perhaps most important was the love and support that Enzokuhle and Amahle developed for each other. Despite the progress made since the end of Apartheid over twenty years earlier, the economic disparity in South Africa between Whites and Blacks made quality of life a still, far-off dream for most. They still did not have equal access to decent education or health care. Amahle's family, part of the growing black middle class, knew that education was especially critical for Blacks with albinism. Amahle stood by Enzokuhle's side to make sure she got the individual help she needed to succeed in school and learn how to make use of opportunities that her family never knew existed.

One day, years later when both girls were high school seniors, they began their walk home after a particularly difficult day of intense reading. Enzokuhle rubbed her fatigued eyes and complained to Amahle, "I'm so tired of being different."

Amahle stopped in her tracks and replied, "Enzokuhle, you need to stop feeling sorry for yourself. Your difference is nothing compared to what you and I have in common. We are both black women. You have to be strong to help me fight for the rights of our brothers and sisters all over our country,"

Enzokuhle stared at her friend. It was another turning

point in Enzokuhle's life. She realized that she had a common purpose with Amahle and thousands of others. She had proved that she could cope with her condition and it was time to move on. The two girls linked arms and began their walk together down the dusty streets of Soweto.

Tanzania

| Abdul and Said |

Abdul awoke to the rooster's crow. "Oh, come on little man, why can't you let me sleep just this once?"

He rubbed his eyes and noticed that he was the only one awake. He glanced around at the other seven bunkbeds; the only sound came from Said, whose incessant snoring continued in its consistent rhythm. Said was a sound sleeper and nothing ever seemed to disturb his slumber. It got to be a game for Abdul every morning. How many times would he have to poke Said to get him out of bed?

It took six pokes this morning, more than usual because it was Saturday and there was no school. Abdul finally got a reaction from his best friend when he reminded Said that after breakfast and their chores, they had planned to go fishing down at the pond, just outside their safe house compound. Tending the chickens was the only Saturday morning chore the two boys were assigned to accomplish together, and they always had a great time doing it, despite the overwhelming smells and disgusting chicken poop they had to clean up. Abdul and Said were both twelve years old and just starting to experience the rush of puberty. The chicken house was a great place to discuss the girls who lived at the safe house without being overheard by anyone else, particularly the headmaster.

"Hey, Said, I think Neema likes you!" Abdul yelled over the din of the thirty or more clucking hens.

Said, who was accustomed to Abdul trying to embarrass him, threw a handful of straw at his friend.

"Ah, shut up Abdul. She doesn't even know I'm alive," he said with a little smile.

Hmm, maybe I should try to make eye contact with Neema in class on Monday, Said thought to himself.

Abdul tried to up the ante with an even bigger taunt. "I saw her looking at the big bulge in your pants the other day at lunch." Abdul laughed as he avoided Said's attempt to tackle him. The pubescent banter continued until the chicken house was clean and the boys had gathered up all the eggs from the nesting boxes. They put on their sunglasses and hats before walking to the kitchen. These eggs would provide a delicious breakfast for all the children in the safe house this morning.

The friendship between Abdul and Said help them cope with their difficult lives behind the walls of the compound. Originally intended to provide security and an education for children with albinism in Tanzania, these safe houses felt more like a prison, and the children who lived there felt they are being punished for being different.

Both Abdul and Said endured trauma and tragedy prior to moving into their safe house. Abdul was abandoned by his mother, who left him in the care of his grandfather. Denied access to an education because his grandfather believed he was "not human," Abdul was forced to work in the fields of his grandfather's farm. When the safe

55

house opened nearby, Abdul was immediately enrolled. He hasn't seen his grandfather since he moved in five years ago.

Said and his younger brother, Emanuel, both had albinism. Their parents moved the family to Dar Es Salaam, hoping to escape the dangers to their children in rural Tanzania, as well as provide an education for the two brothers. One night, a gang of men with machetes broke into their home in the city, and tied up seven-year-old Said and his parents. They kidnapped five-year-old Emanuel and the boy was never heard from again. Soon after the kidnapping, Said was moved to the safe house, which was a four-hour drive away.

Said's parents visit him at his safe house once a year on his birthday, bringing along his new baby sister, who does not have albinism. Like Said, most of the children residing at the safe house suffer from feelings of abandonment. Said dreads the annual visits from his family, which are always awkward. During their visit, the family sits outside in the yard, eating the birthday cake they always bring with them. When his parents ask him about his life in the safe house, Said tries to convince them that he is happy. He talks about his classes, hiding the fact that the itinerant teachers are absent more than they are present. The reality is that Said hates living at the safe house. He misses his old friends and the freedom they all had to play in their neighborhood. He feels trapped like an animal behind the safe house walls.

Most of all, Said misses his little brother. He feels guilty about the kidnapping. *Maybe*, Said tells himself, *the kidnappers would have taken me instead if I had offered myself.* Recurring nightmares of his brother's screams and his mother's sobs on that awful night have haunted Said for years.

During his family's first birthday visit at the safe house, Said asked his parents if they had any news about Emanuel. After a long silence, his mother said only, "We'll never see him again." Then they changed the subject. From that day forward, Said never asked about Emanuel again and this parents talked only about his little sister during their annual visits.

The safe house has few resources to offer the children who live there. Two employees, the headmaster and cook, take care of fifteen children. They cook, clean, and make sure the children are safe and healthy. Once a month, a truck arrives with community donations of fresh vegetables, used books, toys, and clothing to meet the children's day-to-day needs. The government funds a small team of itinerant teachers, who travel among the handful of safe houses throughout Tanzania.

Otherwise, the only assistance for the children comes from international charities. One such charity, Under the Same Sun, provides help to children with albinism throughout Africa, including artificial limbs and sun protection. Recently, a young boy at Abdul and Said's safe house was fitted with an artificial leg to replace the leg severed during an attack by a gang when he lived in a nearby town. Because skin cancer is common among people with albinism, Under the Same Sun also provides sunscreen ointments and annual consultations by a dermatologist at the safe house.

Most of the safe house residents, including Abdul and Said, avoid being outside during the heat of midday. But today Abdul and Said planned to go fishing. After breakfast, while the headmaster was welcoming a group of visitors, the boys slipped out of the back door with the fishing poles they had hidden in the supply room. Quickly, they squeezed under the chain link fence behind the dormitory, through a hole dug by animals.

It was a beautiful day—not too hot. The boys had planned their escape for days. The pond was close by, and Abdul and Said chattered happily as they sat down on some large rocks at water's edge.

The attack happened almost immediately. Abdul was still putting worms on his hook, sitting only a few feet away from his friend, when he heard Said scream. Abdul jerked up his head to see two men with machetes grabbing Said. Abdul leaped up, but his terror prevented him from yelling for help.

One man held Said down while the other hacked off Said's left arm just above the elbow. They ran off, leaving Said in shock, blood pouring from his severed limb. Abdul found his voice and screamed for help. He quickly took off his t-shirt and wrapped it around Said's arm, trying to stem the blood loss. Said slipped into unconsciousness as Abdul dragged him back toward the safe house, continuing his screams as he went.

The headmaster, hearing the commotion, met him at the fence gate and helped Said into the house. He tried to keep Said conscious while Abdul raced to find towels for the boy's bleeding arm. Other children gathered around in horror, staring at their friend, who might be dying in front of them. They waited almost two hours before an ambulance arrived to take Said to the closest hospital— over 50 miles away.

Said survived his attack but his attackers were not caught. During his three weeks at the hospital, Said's severed arm began to heal. Unfortunately, his emotional state did not recover as well. Traumatized and depressed, Said sat listless in a chair, unable or unwilling to make eye contact or engage with his doctors and nurses.

The residents and staff of the safe house were relieved that Said survived his attack. After his return, Abdul hovered over his friend every day. He couldn't stop blaming himself, his thoughts filled with what-ifs. *What if I had been more vigilant to sounds? What if I had been sitting closer to Said? What if I had followed safe house rules and convinced Said that we shouldn't have gone fishing in the first place?* Abdul's usually cheery disposition gradually deteriorated into sullenness and an unwillingness to carry out his chores. The headmaster, concerned at the classic signs of post-traumatic stress, consulted with a social worker from Under the Same Sun about how to help Abdul cope with the trauma of the attack on his friend. The social worker decided to sit down and talk with Abdul.

"How are you feeling about what happened to Said, Abdul?"

For the next thirty minutes, the social worker listened as Abdul shared how he blamed himself for the attack and felt no hope for ever feeling safe outside the walls of the compound.

"Being albino is a curse and I want to die," Abdul said, his voice so low that the social worker had to strain to hear him.

"I don't want to live like a prisoner here but I can't leave. Everyone hates me in the outside world. I wish the attackers had killed me instead of hurting Said."

The story was not unusual; the social worker had heard it many times before in a country where witch doctors continue to promote old superstitions regarding albinism. As a result, many people in rural Tanzania still believe that obtaining the arm, leg, fingers, skin, or hair of a person with albinism and brewing it into a potion will make them rich.

For his part, Said felt that his attack was punishment for not doing enough to save Emanuel from his kidnappers. About a year after his own attack, Said received a prosthetic arm from U.S. doctors affiliated with Under the Same Sun. He slowly began to adjust to both his prosthetic arm and the reality of what people with albinism endure in Tanzania.

Abdul was provided with ongoing counseling from social workers trained by Under the Same Sun. A series of workshops were held in the local community presenting the facts related to albinism. Despite this progress, murders and maiming of people with albinism continue in Tanzania. Without the major cultural change needed to dispel entrenched superstitions about albinism, the government is unable to do much other than build more safe houses. And so, Said, his friend, Abdul, and countless others in Africa still live in isolation with little hope of ever living normal lives.

United Kingdom

| Jack |

Jack hurried down the hall to his first class—algebra. He pushed his thick glasses up closer to his eyes and glanced at his watch; he only had one minute to spare. This was the way most of his mornings began, timing his arrival at school so that most of his classmates were already in the classroom. He was usually the last student to arrive, so he didn't have to endure the taunts in the hallway before class.

Jack pushed his way into his classroom just as his teacher, Mrs. Kiendl, was starting to shut the door. As he walked over to his seat in the front row by the window, he braced himself for what he knew would come.

"Well, here comes Casper the Ghost, late as usual!" shouted William, an obnoxious boy who looked for opportunities to bully Jack every morning. Several of the girls giggled as Jack sat down and adjusted his special magnifying glass that enabled him to read his algebra textbook.

It wasn't the first time that Jack had heard this particular insult. He had a condition called oculocutaneous albinism, which meant that he had little melanin in his skin and hair. He had very pale skin and his hair was pure white. Jack's albinism also affected his eyesight, causing a host of problems, including severe short-sightedness, "lazy eye," and photo-sensitivity. He wore thick glasses most of the time and dark sunglasses whenever he went outside. Because he was legally blind, Jack also had an electronic cane, which he used primarily to navigate the six blocks he walked every day to and from school.

Jack's condition made him look different from the other kids at his secondary school near Birmingham, England. In fact, to his knowledge, Jack was the only student who had albinism at his school. Jack knew from the time he started school that he was different. But he had never felt as alone and miserable as he did now. It almost seemed as if once the kids became teenagers, no one wanted to be his friend. It was all about fitting in and Jack definitely didn't fit in.

Now, as algebra class ended and Jack gathered up his books, he heard another student from a couple of rows back. "Hey Ghost, don't forget your googly eyes." Jack didn't reply but he felt his cheeks burn with embarrassment.

As Jack made his way toward the classroom door, Mrs. Kiendl called after him. "Jack, can I speak with you for a moment?"

Jack turned around and thought for a moment that Mrs. Kiendl was going to reprimand him for being late to class. He certainly didn't expect her next comment.

"Jack, I feel sad when I hear the other kids calling you names. I've also noticed that you don't seem to have many friends here at school—you've been alone every time I've seen you in the hallways. "

63

She paused and when Jack didn't respond, Mrs. Kiendl continued.

"You may not know this but when I was a young girl, I stuttered badly. The other kids used to tease me, which made it worse. It wasn't until I went to speech therapy and met another kid my age that had the same problem that I learned how to cope with the bullying. It helped me a lot to be able to talk about my experience and to feel like someone else cared. I know that words hurt."

Jack didn't know how to respond, so he just said, "Thanks for your concern, Mrs. Kiendl. I've gotten used to the other kids calling me names."

Mrs. Kiendl smiled and said, "Okay, Jack. I just wanted you to know that you can talk to me anytime you want. Bullying is a problem at this school. You're not the only student who has been a victim. Teenagers can be cruel to anyone they perceive to be different, whether it is from appearance, disability, race, or ethnicity. I'm planning an after-school group for any student who feels they've experienced bullying. Do you think this is something you might be interested in?"

By this time, Jack was starting to feel uncomfortable. He replied to Mrs. Kiendl, "I'll think about it. I have to get to my next class. Can you write me a note in case I'm late?"

Despite Jack's discomfort at Mrs. Kiendl's invitation, he did think about it. In fact, it was about all he could think about for the next few days. He thought about how nice it would be to finally get some of his feelings off his chest. But he also wondered if being a part of Mrs. Kiendl's group would just give the school bullies another name to call him: "loser" or "teacher's pet". Maybe it would just be easier to try to ignore the insults or figure out other ways to deal with them.

At dinner the night of his conversation with Mrs. Kiendl, Jack was very quiet. His mum, who worked full-time as a nurse at a nearby health clinic, looked at her son.

"Jack, how was school today? You look a bit gloomy."

"Hunky-dory, Mum," Jack replied, still looking down at his plate.

Jack's mum was as astute as most mothers are about their children. Having grown up in Druid's Heath with an alcoholic father and a mother who was constantly angry, she was probably even more aware than many what it was like to be unhappy. So, she pressed further with her son.

"Did you get bullied again today?"

"Bloody hell, Mum! I get bullied every day!" Jack blurted out.

Jack's dad, a Pakistani immigrant to England, who had settled in Birmingham with his family as a child, looked up.

"You do not speak to your mother that way, Jack. You apologize right now."

"Sorry, Mum, it's just that you and Dad don't understand what I go through every day. The kids call me names and make fun of me all the time. I don't have any friends and I probably never will."

Tears welled up in Jack's eyes and he hastily wiped them away.

Jack's dad said quietly, "No, we don't know what it's like to have albinism. But we both know what it is like to be different and not fit in. When my family first moved here, the other kids in my neighborhood threw rocks at me and told me to move back where I came from. They shouted that I was dirty and evil. Your mother had a terrible time in secondary school because she was poor and didn't have the right clothes. The other girls laughed at her and didn't invite her to their parties. Is that right, Mother?"

"Yes, that's right," Jack's mother said. "I was very lonely and isolated at school until a teacher convinced me to join a club where the members did volunteer work at the local hospital. It was the best decision I ever made. I met wonderful people at the hospital and I made new friends who didn't judge me for my clothes. I wouldn't be a nurse today if I hadn't joined that volunteer group."

A week later, Jack told Mrs. Kiendl that he would like to join the group she was planning. It took a few meetings before the members became comfortable enough to start sharing their experiences and feelings. However, after Jack met Albie and the two of them laughed uproariously over the irony of the boy's name, Jack knew he had at last found a friend. The group soon became the most important part of Jack's life.

Albie had a significant hearing loss and had recently transferred to Jack's school. Jack observed how Albie laughed off the taunts of their classmates. Jack began to feel more self-confident in the face of bullying. He discovered that Albie was learning to play the drums even though he couldn't hear much of the sound.

Inspired by Albie's determination, Jack decided that he wanted to join the rowing team, despite the bright sunshine that was often the reality of outdoor events on the river. With sunscreen to protect his skin and special sunglasses to shield his eyes, Jack had no trouble fitting in with the lads on his rowing team. He discovered a passion, as well as talent for the popular sport, and it ultimately resulted in a university scholarship.

Despite the despair he often felt in secondary school, Jack now feels positive about his future. He hopes to become an ophthalmologist one day. Thanks to supportive family, dedicated teachers, and like-minded friends, Jack is confident that he will succeed.

United States

| Angie |

You could hear the chants from two blocks away. "Black Lives Matter! Stop police brutality!" The protesters seemed to be getting closer.

Angie turned to her friend, Patrice. "What should we do?"

Patrice looked uncertain. "I'm not sure. Mama told me to stay clear of the protests because she's afraid I'll get hurt."

"Well, I want to join them," Angie replied, "but I need you to stay with me. The protesters will accept me better if I'm with a black person."

Patrice looked at Angie and laughed. "Yeah, you're about as white as it gets. But I don't think any of those dudes would kick you out. Black people have been trying to get white people riled up for racial justice forever and from what I hear, there are a lot of white kids from the university who are marching."

Angie nodded and thought about Patrice's perception that she would be regarded as any other white person joining in the protest. She wasn't sure about that. Patrice didn't understand that having albinism pretty much made you an outcast of any group.

Angie and Patrice had been best friends since the third grade when, at the age of eight, Angie didn't see herself as different from the other girls in her class. But one day in class her teacher asked everyone to get out a pencil for their math lesson. Angie immediately realized that she had left her pencil bag at home. She looked up in alarm, not knowing what to do. As her teacher distributed the math worksheets, she saw that Angie was on the verge of tears because she didn't have a pencil.

"Who can lend Angie a pencil?" the teacher asked the class. Immediately, all the other students turned to look at Angie. Angie wanted to die. No one offered a pencil. One other girl snickered, "I bet she is as dumb as she looks."

Then Patrice, the only black girl in the class, jumped up from her desk in the back corner and brought over a pencil to Angie. "Don't worry. You can bring it back to me tomorrow."

From that day on, Angie and Patrice had been best friends. Since there were so few black students in their school and Angie was the only student with albinism, their friendship was a godsend to them both. The other girls tended to group themselves into cliques and the boys were just loud and gross. None of the other students reached out to Angie or Patrice.

But Angie and Patrice had each other and that was enough. Now, at age fourteen, they knew everything there was to know about each other—or so they thought. Angie was an only child and neither of her parents had albinism. They worried about her incessantly—was she able to see the blackboard? Did she wear her hat when she was on the playground? Were other children kind to her? Her parents, both nurses, educated themselves and their daughter about her genetic condition and they met

69

with school officials at the beginning of each school year to make sure her needs were met. Middle school brought fresh social challenges however, and Angie keenly felt her differences from the other girls. She often felt that the other white girls whispered about her and grew silent when she came close. Patrice always had her back though, and Angie felt safe. As the girls grew older, Angie grew more introverted, balancing her life among school, reading books about horses and dogs, and spending time with Patrice.

Patrice came from a different family background than Angie's. She was the youngest of three children raised by their single mother. While money was always tight, love was never in short supply. Patrice's two older brothers protected her from the rough kids in their neighborhood and they helped her with schoolwork. When they were old enough to get part time jobs, they both worked after school, eager to help with Patrice's voice lessons. Everyone said that Patrice would be the next Aretha Franklin, and Angie loved listening to her best friend practice.

Today, Angie and Patrice linked arms and headed in the direction of the protest. As the sun set, the protest seemed to get louder and more intense. When the girls reached the crowd, they were surprised to see a variety of people – Black, white, brown, male and female, young and old—even a small group of what looked like war veterans in wheelchairs. The air was thick with the smell of tear gas, and visibility was decreasing rapidly from smoke.

Angie's poor vision made it difficult for her to see beyond the edge of the crowd, but she was excited to be part of what she instinctively knew was an important event.

Patrice shouted over the din. "Look, Angie, there's my voice teacher! She is up at the front. I'll be right back."

She let go of Angie's arm and started weaving through the crowd to reach her teacher.

Angie lost sight of her friend and started to panic at the prospect of being left alone in the chaos growing in the crowd. As she squinted through her thick glasses and tried to locate Patrice, she saw two men break the windows of a nearby police patrol car, reach in and grab two automatic rifles. They sprinted in the same direction Angie last saw Patrice. Suddenly shots rang out and people started running in all directions. Someone ran into Angie, knocking her down. She reached for her glasses, which were shattered and lying on the street a foot away.

Without her glasses and Patrice nowhere in sight, Angie felt helpless. She heard ambulance sirens and she screamed, "Patrice, where are you?" No answer from the best friend whom Angie had relied upon for years.

Suddenly, Angie felt a tight grip on her arm. She whipped around, but without her glasses, could only see the form of a tall woman with flowing white hair and thick glasses.

"Come with me, honey. You're not safe out here."

The woman led Angie over to the sidewalk and they

walked carefully together while everyone else raced past them to safety. When they reached an area Angie recognized vaguely as the entrance to a local church, they stopped and the woman said, "What's your name and who were you yelling for?"

"My name is Angie and my friend, Patrice, went up to the front of the protest to see her voice teacher. I'm so worried about her."

The woman put an arm around the trembling Angie and said softly, "Well, you are safe now, Angie, and we'll ask a policeman to find your friend. By the way, I see that you have albinism and that you can't see well without your glasses. My name is Mary Walls and I also have albinism. We can support one another until my friend, Bob, can reach us. We'll make sure you get home safely."

It wasn't long before a police car pulled up to the church entrance and asked if Mary and Angie needed help. He stayed with them until Bob arrived, using the time to inform Angie about what happened to Patrice. To Angie's horror, Patrice had been in the line of fire between the police and the men who had stolen the rifles. She was hit in the shoulder by a police bullet and had been taken by ambulance to the local hospital. Apparently, the wound was not life-threatening.

Angie was grounded by her parents for a month for attending the protest with Patrice without permission. Instead of hanging out with Patrice, Angie used her time at home to text with her new friend, Mary Walls. Mary took Angie under her wing and introduced her online to the organization, National Organization for Albinism and Hypopigmentation (NOAH). NOAH had a division for teenagers, and for the first time, Angie became friends with others like herself. She was astonished to find other people who didn't let their albinism limit their interests, skills, or aspirations. She learned to feel good about her differences and abilities. She began to recognize that everyone is different in some way from each other. While she and Patrice had always shared a feeling of being outsiders in their school, Angie's growing self-confidence led her to value Patrice as a talented and loyal friend more than as her protector. They both widened their circles of friends and their friendship with each other flourished as well.

Years later, when both girls were seniors in high school, Patrice passed Angie in the hallway and yelled out excitedly, "Hey Angie, guess what? I got a gig singing with a band!"

Angie beamed at her friend and replied, "Congratulations! And I have news for you too! I got a summer job at the veterinarian's office just down the street!"

Life is good when you're different.

What Is The Truth About Albinism?

Introduction

Albinism is a complex, inherited, genetic condition that affects the amount of melanin the body produces. Melanin controls the pigmentation of one's skin, eyes and hair. People with albinism typically have pale skin, eyes, and hair, but they don't all look alike and their experiences are different.

What Causes Albinism?

People are born with albinism because they inherit one or more albinism gene(s) from their parents. Several genes provide instructions for making proteins involved in the production of melanin. Melanin is produced by cells called melanocytes, which are found in your skin, hair and eyes.

Albinism is caused by a mutation in one of these genes. Different types of albinism can occur, based mainly on which gene caused the disorder. The mutation may result in no melanin at all or a significantly reduced amount of melanin.

What are the Myths and Facts about Albinism?

Myth: PWAs don't mind being called albinos.

Fact: Opinions vary on the use of the word albino. While

some find it offensive, others feel the label carries neutral or even empowering connotations. PWAs agree that their feelings depend on the intent in which the word is used. The term can be derogatory when said mockingly, or it can be used innocently by someone who means no offense or is just curious.

Myth: Albinism is a disease.
Fact: Albinism is a genetic condition, not a disease. It is inherited through families. People born with albinism inherit an albinism gene from their parents.

Myth: Albinism is a result of evil or witchery.
Fact: Albinism reduces the amount of melanin pigment formed in the skin, hair, and or eyes. The "evil albino" stereotype or portrayal of PWAs in film and fiction often reinforces societal prejudice and discrimination.

Myth: The body parts of those with albinism have superpowers.
Fact: In some African countries, hundreds of children with albinism are maimed or murdered each year because their body parts are believed to bring good fortune and wealth to those who possess them.

Myth: Albinism is contagious.
Fact: Because albinism is a genetic condition, it cannot be "caught" from anyone.

Myth: Albinism can result when a black woman is impregnated by a white man.

Fact: While albinism is a genetic condition, it has nothing to do with the genetics of race.

Myth: Albinism is caused by a lack of exposure to the sun.

Fact: This is a dangerous misconception. Exposure to the sun places the PWA at a higher risk for skin cancer.

Myth: All PWAs have pink or red eyes.

Fact: Lighting conditions can allow the blood vessels at the back of the eye to be seen, which can cause the eyes to look pink or violet. However most PWAs have blue eyes, and some have hazel or brown eyes.

Myth: Albinism only occurs in ethnic Africans.

Fact: Albinism's prevalence worldwide is approximately 1:20,000. Albinism occurs at a higher rate of approximately 1:4,000 in some African countries, including Zimbabwe and Tanzania.

Myth: All PWAs are blind.

Fact: The degree of vision impairment varies with the different types of albinism. However, PWAs all have vision problems that are not completely correctable with eyeglasses, and many have low vision. Vision problems in PWAs are caused by the abnormal development of the retina and the abnormal patterns of nerve connections between the eye and the brain. The presence of these eye problems defines a diagnosis of albinism.

Myth: People with albinism have shorter life expectancies than those without the condition.
Fact: Most PWAs can live normal life spans if they have access to adequate skin protection, such as sunscreens rated 20 SPF or higher, and opaque clothing.

Myth: Albinism is well-understood around the world.
Fact: PWAs are at risk of isolation because the condition is often misunderstood. Social stigma—in the form of bullying—is common, especially within communities of color, or where race and culture contribute to stereotypes and misinformation.

Myth: PWAs all have pure white skin and hair.
Fact: Most PWAs have fair complexions, but skin and hair color vary with the different types of albinism. A person with albinism may have white, shades of blonde, light brown, or red hair.

Myth: PWAs will have children with albinism.
Fact: If both parents carry the gene, there's a 1 in 4 chance their child will inherit albinism and a 1 in 2 chance their child will be a carrier. Carriers do not have albinism but can pass on the gene.

Myth: People who do not have albinism cannot have a child with albinism.

Fact: A person who carries the gene may not have albinism, but can pass on the gene.

Myth: Laws and policies protect PWAS.

Fact: Superstition and ignorance fuel the physical and emotional dangers to PWAs. Many countries do not define albinism as a disability, and therefore do not provide adaptive devices for those with low vision in school, or even sunscreen lotion. Also, many PWAs exist in extreme poverty, unable to find jobs due to discrimination and lack of government funding.

Myth: DNA tests can identify conclusively what kind of albinism an individual has.

Fact: There is no simple test to determine whether a person carries a gene for albinism. Researchers have analyzed the DNA of many PWAs and found the genetic changes that cause albinism, but these changes are not always in exactly the same place, even for a given type of albinism. Moreover, many of the tests do not find all possible genetic changes. Therefore, the tests for the albinism gene may be inconclusive.

For specific information and genetic testing, it is important to seek the advice of a qualified geneticist or genetic counselor. The American College of Medical

Genetics and the National Society of Genetic Counselors maintain a referral list.

What are the Types of Albinism?

There are four general types of albinism:
1. Oculocutaneous albinism
2. Ocular albinism
3. Hermansky-Pudlak syndrome
4. Chediak-Higashi syndrome

Oculocutaneous albinism (OCA) is the most common type of albinism. People with OCA have pale hair, skin, and eyes. OCA is actually a group of inherited genetic conditions characterized by a reduction in or complete lack of melanin pigment in the skin, hair, and eyes. These conditions are caused by gene mutations in specialized cells called melanocytes that produce the melanin pigment. Insufficient melanin pigment results in abnormal development of the eyes, resulting in vision abnormalities, and light skin that is susceptible to damage from the sun including skin cancer.

Visual changes include nystagmus (involuntary side-to-side eye movement), strabismus (one eye is turned in a direction that is different from the other eye) and photophobia (sensitivity to light). Other changes include foveal hypoplasia (which affects visual acuity) and misrouting of the optic nerves. All individuals with OCA have the above visual changes but the amount of skin, hair, and iris pigment can vary depending on the gene (or type of OCA) and mutation involved.

Research on albinism genes is ongoing. Seven forms of oculocutaneous albinism are now recognized: OCA1, OCA2, OCA3, OCA4, OCA5, OCA6, and OCA7. Each type of OCA is discussed below.

- OCA1 results from a genetic defect in an enzyme called tyrosinase. This enzyme helps the body to change the amino acid, tyrosine, into pigment. The frequency of OCA1 is approximately 1/40,000 in the world population. There are two subtypes of OCA1.

  - OCA1A – The enzyme is inactive and no melanin is produced leading to white hair and very light skin.

  - OCA1B – The enzyme is minimally active and a small amount of melanin is produced, leading to hair that may darken to blond, yellow/orange, or even light brown, as well as slightly more pigment in the skin.

- OCA2, or P gene albinism, is the most common type of albinism and is caused by mutation of the P gene. People with OCA2 generally have more pigment and better vision than those with OCA1, but cannot tan like someone with OCA1b. Some pigment can develop into freckles or moles. People with OCA2 usually have fair skin, but are usually not as pale as OCA1. They have pale blonde to golden, strawberry blonde, or even brown hair, and most commonly blue eyes. Affected people of African descent usually have a different phenotype (appearance): yellow hair; pale skin; and blue, gray, or hazel eyes. The prevalence of OCA2 in most populations is approximately 1/38,000-1/40,000.

- OCA3 has been only partially researched. It is the result of a mutation of the tyrosinase-related protein 1 gene. Reported in Africa and New Guinea, individuals with OCA3 typically have red hair, reddish-brown skin, and blue or gray eyes. The incidence rate of OCA3 is unknown.

- OCA4 is rare outside Japan, where it accounts for 24% of all albinism cases. It is caused by a genetic defect in the SLC45A2 protein that helps the tyrosinase enzyme to function. People with OCA4 produce a minimal amount of melanin, similar to people with OCA2.

- OCA5 was identified only in one Pakistani family with golden-colored hair, white skin, nystagmus, photophobia, foveal hypoplasia, and impaired visual acuity. It is caused by a defect in human chromosome region 4q24, but analysis failed to identify a candidate gene.

- OCA6 is also one of the rarest forms of OCA. It was detected in Chinese individuals but is not believed to be limited to Chinese ethnicity. OCA6 varies in its effect on hair color, and results from mutations in the

SLC24A5 gene.

- OCA7 was first identified in a family from the Faroe Islands, and later in a Lithuanian patient. OCA7 is characterized by lighter pigmentation and significant effects on visual acuity. It is due to a gene mutation in C10orf11, a gene of unknown function.

Ocular Albinism (OA) is much less common than OCA. It affects only the eyes. People with OA usually have blue eyes. Sometimes the irises (the colored part of the eyes) are very pale, causing the eyes to appear red or pink. This is because the blood vessels inside the eyes show through the irises. The skin and hair color are usually normal.

OA is caused by a change in the GPR143 gene that plays a signaling role and is especially important to pigmentation in the eye. OA follows a simpler pattern of inheritance because the gene for OA is on the X chromosome. Females have two copies of the X chromosome while males have only one copy (and a Y chromosome that makes them male). To have ocular albinism, a male only needs to inherit one changed copy of the gene for ocular albinism from his carrier mother. Therefore almost all people with OA are males. Parents should be suspicious if a female child is said to have ocular albinism. While it is possible if the mother is a carrier of ocular albinism and the father has ocular albinism, it is extremely rare.

In all types of OCA and some types of OA, albinism is passed on in an autosomal recessive inheritance pattern. This means a child has to get two copies of the gene that causes albinism (one from each parent) to have the condition.

Hermansky-Pudlak Syndrome (HPS) is a type of albinism that includes a form of OCA along with blood disorders; bruising problems; and lung, kidney, or bowel diseases.

The skin, hair, and eyes of a person with HPS may vary in color from very pale to almost normal. Eyesight is usually impaired, commonly with visual acuities of 20/200 or worse. The blood storage abnormality associated with HBS may cause excessive bleeding, especially in women during menstruation. Bleeding may become life-threatening, and aspirin makes the bleeding worse. Approximately one-sixth of HPS patients develop inflammation of the colon, with bleeding. Some forms of HPS can cause a lung disease called pulmonary fibrosis that can lead to death.

Chediak-Higashi Syndrome (CHS) is a rare inherited complex immune disorder that usually occurs in childhood. It is characterized by reduced pigment in the skin and eyes (oculocutaneous albinism), immune deficiency with an increased susceptibility to infections, and a tendency to bruise and bleed easily. Neurological deficits are also common. CHS is transmitted as an autosomal recessive genetic condition.

CHS affects males and females in equal numbers. It is often obvious at birth or shortly thereafter. There does not appear to be a higher risk for any particular ethnic or racial group. There are less than 500 cases of the disease on record.

What are the symptoms of albinism?

To summarize our discussion of the symptoms of the various types of albinism, the skin of a PWA often appears pale white, cream, or pink. People with ocular albinism may have skin that is brown or otherwise similar to the color of their relatives without albinism.

Some children born with albinism may start or speed up production of melanin as they grow into their teens. Their skin may turn a bit darker. PWAs can burn easily in the sun and are more likely to get skin cancer, some as early as in their teens.

The eyesight of someone with albinism is affected by the lack of melanin. Melanin is critical for the development of optic nerves that enable one to focus on images like printed words and faces. Even with glasses or contacts, the problem cannot be corrected to normal vision. Less color in the eyes causes vision to be worse.

Signs of albinism may not be easily visible in everyone. Issues with eyesight may be the first clue that someone may have the condition. These symptoms include:

- Eyes that are sensitive to light (called photosensitivity)
- Eyes that move quickly or uncontrollably
- Eyes that are crossed
- A "lazy eye" (called strabismus)
- Back and forth movement of the eyes (called nystagmus)
- Problem seeing things close up (farsightedness) or in the distance (nearsightedness)

The hair of someone with albinism can range from very white, yellow, or even reddish. As one gets older, their hair may darken to blond or even light brown.

How Is Albinism Treated?

Most PWAs are otherwise healthy. Treatments mainly include taking care of the eyes and skin. To care for the eyes, PWAs should:

- see an ophthalmologist (eye doctor) regularly for initial diagnosis and ongoing treatment for nystagmus, strabismus, and other eye problems.
- wear special glasses or contact lenses to protect their eyes from the sun

PWAs have an increased risk of developing skin cancer. To protect their skin, they can:

- wear broad-spectrum sunscreen with at least SPF 30 when going outside and reapply every 2 hours
- try to stay in the shade as much as possible

- cover up with clothing with SPF protection
- wear a hat
- check their skin regularly for changes or suspicious marks
- see their dermatologist every six to twelve months for a skin check
- avoid tanning beds
- avoid medicines that increase sun sensitivity

What Else Should I Know?

Learn all you can about albinism. The care team is a great resource. You also can find information and support online at: National Organization for Albinism and Hypopigmentation (NOAH).

Because the social scene can be more about fitting in than standing out, people with albinism may face bullying or prejudice. Voicing any frustration or sadness to a family member or friend who understands can help. So can talking to a counselor or therapist to get ideas on coping with any challenges.

Resources

What Is Albinism?

This section provides a variety of resources to help the reader understand albinism, its symptoms, consequences, and treatments. While the list of citations is lengthy, it is not meant to be intimidating. Those citations below that are numbered may be sufficient to answer most questions about albinism.

1. www.albinism.org/about-albinism

2. www.albinism.org/resourcelibrary/

3. https://news.un.org/en/story/2013/05/438822-persons-albinism-must-not-be-treated-ghosts-un-experts-stress

4. www.ohchr.org/Documents/Issues/Albinism/Albinism_Worldwide_Report2021_EN.pdf

5. Many people with albinism agree that their feelings regarding the use of the word, albino, depend on the context or intent in which the word is used. https://bit.ly/3H6k8Jp

6. www.albinism.org/information-bulletin-low-vision-aids/

7. www.albinism.org/information-bulletin-social-aspects-of-albinism/

8. https://rarediseases.org/rare-diseases/oculocutaneous-albinism/

9. At Under the Same Sun, members advocate for the phrase "person with albinism" instead of Albino, because it puts the person ahead of their condition. https://bit.ly/3JLs9p0

www.un.org/en/observances/albinism-day

https://my.clevelandclinic.org/health/diseases/21747-albinism

In this exploratory study, research was conducted by interviewing four people with albinism in Africa to get an understanding of the social discrimination they faced. https://bit.ly/3s6lOyn

Google home page for treatment of albinism: https://bit.ly/33BHEAb

Website for Hadley.edu where the mission of the organization is to create personalized learning opportunities that empower adults with vision loss or blindness to thrive. https://bit.ly/3h4CvUo

www.healthline.com/health/albinism

https://kidshealth.org/en/teens/albinism.html

www.nationalgeographic.com/magazine/2017/06/albinism-health-genetics-society/

www.mayoclinic.org/diseases-conditions/albinism/symptoms-causes/syc-20369184

An article that addresses how black people with albinism see their identities in their families, communities, and the world. https://n.pr/3p3XcEB

A slide presentation from Under the Same Sun that addresses the global social stigma facing persons with albinism. https://bit.ly/3IaasyG

"11 Things To Remember If You Love A Person With Albinism" by Bethany Rosselit http://parentofchildwithalbinism.com

https://rarediseases.org/rare-diseases/ocular-albinism/

https://rarediseases.org/rare-diseases/hermansky-pudlak-syndrome/

https://rarediseases.org/rare-diseases/chediak-higashi-syndrome/

"What Is Albinism?" by Under the Same Sun can be found here: https://bit.ly/3h8bz64

"Protecting Children with Albinism from Bullying" https://underthesamesun.com/sites/default/files/Bullying.pdf

www.webmd.com/skin-problems-and-treatments/what-is-albinism

https://en.wikipedia.org/wiki/Oculocutaneous_albinism

https://en.wikipedia.org/wiki/Albinism_in_popular_culture

"Breaking Myths About Albinism" by ALBA can be found on YouTube: https://bit.ly/3BMh3gt

PWAs experience their condition differently depending on where they live. The citations in the following section are grouped by the specific country that is the basis for each short story in this book.

Australia

https://albinismaustralia.org

An article about a conference in Australia that aims to bust myths about albinism. https://ab.co/33BmcLE

An article about Dr Shari Parker, Medical Practitioner and Rehabilitation Physician, President of the World Albinism Alliance, and Secretary of the Albinism Fellowship of Australia. https://bit.ly/3h0UjzZ

This article addresses the isolated western Java village of Ciburuy, which has one of the highest rates of albinism in Indonesia, and nobody seems to know why. https://ab.co/3LP8zdi

https://www.mamamia.com.au/kids-living-with-albinism/

Fiji has one of the highest rates of people with albinism in the world yet very little is known about it by locals. This article addresses the struggles they endure. https://bit.ly/358yw6B

https://www.studiesinaustralia.com/studying-in-australia/living-in-australia/aussie-slang

https://www.thatslife.com.au/aussie-mum-dont-stare-at-my-albino-girls

A fact sheet about albinism from Vision Australia. The focus is on the vision problems of persons with albinism. https://bit.ly/3JzngiC

Brazil

Interview with a family in Brazil in which three of the six children have albinism. https://bit.ly/3Ib927b

https://www.theguardian.com/music/2020/dec/07/brazil-is-a-racist-country-statistically-luedji-luna-the-bold-voice-of-bahia

https://www.ohchr.org/EN/NewsEvents/Pages/DisplayNews.aspx?NewsID=25250&LangID=E

This article addresses the discrimination that persons with albinism face in Brazil. Discrimination often starts at home due to a lack of knowledge about albinism. https://bit.ly/3s8oeg0

https://tiphero.com/three-albino-children

https://unframed.lacma.org/2015/04/22/why-albino-some-notes-our-new-casta-painting-miguel-cabrera

Canada

www.albinism.org/resourcelibrary/

https://albinism.ohchr.org/story-peter-ash.html

www.albinism.org/teen-spotlight-alisha-l/

www.ctvnews.ca/canada/singled-out-police-question-man-with-albinism-who-didn-t-look-like-son-1.2821222

www.youtube.com/watch?v=A6zh7JG-FsI

China

https://abilitymagazine.com/china-love-and-albinism/

www.bbc.com/news/world-asia-china-56464881

An article on food traditions in Chongqing, China: https://bit.ly/36yUEId

www.ohchr.org/Documents/HRBodies/HRCouncil/AdvisoryCom/Albinism/Chinese_Organization_for_Albinism.pdf

www.pilotonline.com/news/article_268f4424-fd69-5d70-8b4b-efde24c6f2c5.html

https://psuchina.wordpress.com/2012/07/19/life-as-a-pedestrian-in-chongqing/

www.travelchinaguide.com/attraction/beijing/qianmen-street.htm

Guna, Panama

www.algazeera.com/indepth/inpictures/indigenous-gun-living-albinism-panama-190730144647964.html

www.efe.com/efe/english/life/panama-s-guna-an-indigenous-group-with-ultra-high-rates-of-albinism/50000263-4017014

www.pinterest.com/pin/290552613437078555/

A pictorial essay about the experiences, myths, and beliefs of the albino population in Guna, Panama. https://bit.ly/35dY8PF

Hong Kong

https://nextshark.com/connie-chiu-meet-the-worlds-first-albino-fashion-model-from-hong-kong/

A successful judo athlete does not let his poor vision, a consequence of his condition of albinism, deter him. https://bit.ly/33FVim2

"Albinism Awareness Campaign" by the UN Human Rights can be found on YouTube: https://bit.ly/351e3Ru

India

www.hindustantimes.com/static/groundglass/albino-delhi-single-out-family/

https://janvikassamiti.org/wp-content/uploads/2020/08/Albinism%20in%20India_A%20Situation%20Analysis.pdf

www.newyorker.com/culture/photo-booth/a-photographer-documents-the-secluded-lives-of-his-aunts

www.thebetterindia.com/50960/jeevan-trust-albinism-awareness/

Israel

www.haaretz.com/1.5176851

www.hadassah.org/story/children-with-low-vision-receive-unique-care-at-hadassah

Positive perceptions about persons with albinism in Israel are described in this article by *The Jerusalem Post.* https://bit.ly/36nLhe5

www.jpost.com/middle-east/persons-with-albinism-in-the-mena-region-fight-for-their-rights-670853

South Africa

Persons with albinism in southern Africa are especially vulnerable to the effects of COVID-19. https://bit.ly/3BRkTVT

www.scielo.org.za/scielo.php?script=sci_arttext&pid=S1996-20962017000100007

www.thesouthafrican.com/news/albinos-murders-south-africa-why/

Tanzania

An investigation into the impact of stigma on the education and life opportunities available to children and young people with albinism in Tanzania and Uganda. https://bit.ly/3p5onyz

www.elsevier.com/books/albinism-in-africa/kromberg/978-0-12-813316-3

www.jaad.org/article/S0190-9622(15)00237-6/pdf

www.latimes.com/world/africa/la-fg-malawi-albinos-hunted-2017-story.html

www.ncbi.nlm.nih.gov/pmc/articles/PMC6185843/

www.underthesamesun.com/content/issue#superstition-and-witchcraft

www.voanews.com/africa/women-living-albinism-struggle-find-good-job#

www.abc.net.au/news/2015-01-15/tanzania-bans-witch-doctors-to-deter-albino-killings/6017938

United Kingdom

A study of the characteristics of bullying in schools in the United Kingdom. https://bit.ly/3BETbvp

www.bbc.com/news/newsbeat-54931351

www.birminghammail.co.uk/whats-on/whats-on-news/14-things-you-only-know-9742256

An article about the financially and social deprived area of Druids Heath, a segment of Birmingham, England. https://bit.ly/3JLPhDt

A list of British slang terms. https://bit.ly/3p7mT71

www.tandem.net/british-slang-words

United States

www.albinism.org/resourcelibrary/

https://aapos.org/glossary/albinism

https://scholarworks.gsu.edu/cgi/viewcontent.cgi?article=1130&context=anthro_theses

An article by ABC News called "Fighting The Stigma of Albinism" can be found here: https://abcn.ws/3JPv6Vn

A university research study about social discrimination against persons with albinism in the United States. https://bit.ly/3Hem0A0

www.vice.com/en/article/pamkan/what-growing-up-as-a-black-albino-taught-me

Organizations that Support People with Albinism

National Organization for Albinism and Hypopigmentation (NOAH)
PO Box 959
East Hempstead, NH 03826-0959
Phone: (603) 887-2310
Toll-free: (800) 473-2310
Email: info@albinism.org
Website: http://www.albinism.org

Under The Same Sun
#303 - 15127 100th Avenue
Surrey, B.C. Canada
V3R 0N9
Email: info@underthesamesun.com

Other Organizations

Albinism Fellowship
P.O. Box 77
Burnley
Lancashire, BB11 5GN United Kingdom
Phone: (791) 954-3518
Toll-free: 447919543518
Email: support@albinism.org.uk
Website: http://www.albinism.org.uk

American Foundation for the Blind
1401 South Clark Street
Arlington, Virginia
https://www.afb.org/

Genetic and Rare Diseases (GARD) Information Center
PO Box 8126
Gaithersburg, MD 20898-8126
Phone: (301) 251-4925
Toll-free: (888) 205-2311
Website: http://rarediseases.info.nih.gov/GARD/

March of Dimes
1550 Crystal Dr, Suite 1300
Arlington, VA 22202 USA
Phone: (888) 663-4637
Website: http://www.marchofdimes.org

National Eye Institute
Information Office
31 Center Drive MSC 2510
Bethesda, MD 20892-2510
Phone: 301-496-5248 — English and Spanish
2020@nei.nih.gov

National Federation of the Blind
200 East Wells Street at Jernigan Place
Baltimore, MD 21230
Phone: 410-659-9314
Fax: 410-685-5653
Email: nfb@nfb.org

NIH/National Institute of Child Health and Human Development
31 Center Dr
Building 31, Room 2A32
Bethesda, MD 20892
Toll-free: (800) 370-2943
Email: NICHDInformationResourceCenter@mail.nih.gov
Website: http://www.nichd.nih.gov/